The Road not Taken

NC BARTON

THE ROAD NOT TAKEN

A FRIENDS TO LOVERS CHRISTMAS ROADTRIP ROMANCE

FORTUNE FALLS
BOOK 3

NC BARTON

CHAPTER 1

As my best friend in the whole world sits barefoot on my floor, neon-green margarita in hand, eyes nearly swollen shut with tears, I wonder when I became such a heartless bitch.

She arrived at my house two hours ago, sobbing because, on her way to pick up chips for our regular Margs and Meg third Tuesday of the month (where we drink too much tequila and watch Meg Ryan movies), she passed her boyfriend in his car in the back of the parking lot, his seat leaned back, his eyes closed. She walked up to knock on the window playfully, flirty, and then she saw *her*. She saw all of it. His hot coworker, who he insisted nothing was going on with, was giving him head, right there in the parking lot.

And as she told me all of this over the course of two margaritas, I thought, of course. Of course, he's a cheating, lying piece of shit. Despite the fact that I've always had a weird feeling about her now ex, even if this hadn't happened, something would have. He would've gotten bored, or she would've. They would fight over future children they don't have. Or which streaming service they should drop to save money. Someone would've gotten sick. Something always happens to make a relationship end, which is why I don't do relationships.

But I am not a complete asshole, so I'm keeping those thoughts to myself. I pull my mass of blonde curls up into a messy bun on top of my head. The last notes of "A Thousand Years" play on Heather's phone. She taps the screen, and it starts over for the fifth time. *Fifth.* It's time to intervene.

"Honey, maybe we should—"

Heather hums over me.

I snatch the phone off the black-and-white tiled floor. My hair escapes its bun and gets in my face as I do. I toss it back over my shoulder and move to the other side of the kitchen island. After a few clicks, "I Forgot That You Existed" blasts out of the tiny phone speaker. Enough wallowing. It's time to get mad.

"Ruby McVeigh! Give me my phone back."

"Only if you agree we're moving on to the empowering women playlist. No more sad songs."

"I'm not ready to move on. I don't want to move on." Heather slumps back onto the floor. We've been friends since kindergarten. This is not the first breakup we've waded through together, but I've never seen her this dejected. Guilt prickles my chest. I shouldn't be dictating how this goes.

I sit next to her, the cold December air making the kitchen tile freezing even through my jeans, and put a hand on her knee. "You'll find someone else, someone better."

Heather looks up at me, silent tears running down her face. "I don't want someone else. I don't want someone better. I want him." She brings what's left of her margarita to her mouth and says so quietly I almost don't hear her, "You wouldn't understand."

Her words pack an unexpected sting. I *do* understand. Kind of. I know heartbreak, just not really of the romantic variety. Which is on purpose. I am careful. I have rules. I protect myself—and others, really—from it.

A fire sparks in my belly, partly tequila, but mostly bloodlust. I want to pummel her ex. Saying that won't help right now. Instead, I pat her knee. "I get it. Really, I do, but he's such a prick. You're better off."

"I'm not." Heather stumbles to her feet again, shaking her head so hard, I worry she might be doing some damage. "You can't possibly understand. You're always doing the dumping."

She's drunk, drunker than I realized, and now she's lashing out. I'm a thirty-two-year-old woman. Of course, I've been dumped. Haven't I? And anyway, it's not like I dumped them exactly. We both agreed to just have fun, and that's exactly what we did. No labels. No hard feelings.

"No one was dumped. If you don't take it all so seriously, then no one gets hurt. And if no one gets hurt, then everyone has fun."

Heather shakes her head. "Some of your beaus didn't get the memo. You may think it all didn't mean anything, but they were left heartbroken." Her voice catches on the last word, and she doubles over, clutching her stomach, her shoulders shaking with sobs.

I really don't think that's true. But there's no time to argue about this right now. I hop up off the floor and wrap her in a big hug. "Let's order a pizza and watch Meg."

We were going to watch *The Women*, but since Meg catches her husband cheating, that's out. *Innerspace* it is.

Heather lays her head on my shoulder. "And open some wine?"

Not a good idea, but the girl's been through trauma.

"Sure. This will all feel better in the morning."

THE LIGHT IS TOO bright as it streams in through the single-pane living room windows. The air is practically Siberian. This house used to be my grandmother's, and before that it was *her* grandmother's. There have been some updates, but some is still original. Like the hardwood floors, the tile in the bathroom, and unfortunately, the windows.

I sit up and stretch my neck, each vertebra popping as I do. I'm not sure if Heather is going to feel better when she wakes up, but I really don't. Red wine and tequila do not mix. When will I learn?

Heather is on the other side of my oversize couch, snuggled in the blanket nest we made last night. I get up and make my way to the kitchen, the massive bay window making the light even brighter in here. The tile is so cold under my bare feet that I wince as I put some grounds into the filter and fill the machine with water.

Small whirs and gurgles of the coffee percolating warm my heart. A shame it can't warm my feet. I sit at the yellow kitchen table, watching the snow fall lightly outside the window and running my hand along the smooth Formica. This table also used to be my grandmother's and has sat in this corner by the window for as long as I can remember. When she passed, my mother suggested I spruce up the place, get some new furniture. But I couldn't bring myself to get rid of Grandma's stuff. She loved this house, this table. Even her clothes are still hanging in the closet of her untouched bedroom.

The snow is picking up speed as I go to pour myself a mug of coffee. Hopefully, it doesn't snow too much, or walking to my shift at the bar later will take a lot longer than usual. I take my coffee back to the blanket nest, turning on an episode of *The Great British Bake Off*. I try to zone out on the intricacies of puff pastry, but Heather's words from last night keep nagging at me.

After the second episode, I can't sit still anymore. I shove my feet into my fuzzy suede slippers and go back to the kitchen. I put a saucepan on the stove, pouring in milk and heat butter. I've made this recipe so many times, I know it by heart. Once the butter is fully incorporated, I pour the mixture into a bowl, testing the heat with my pinky. Feels right to me. I scoop out some yeast and set the timer on my phone for ten minutes. The snow is still falling steadily.

Heather is wrong. All the men I've dated felt the same way I did. We were having fun until we weren't. We parted ways, no hard feelings. Except maybe a few. Mentally, I start tallying up my relationships but am barely past tenth grade when my timer dings.

Adding the flour half a cup at a time, I stir until my spatula gets stuck. Then I start to knead. The dough is firm and squishy in my hands. My muscles in my biceps turn on. It's all so familiar and soothing. But my mind is still swirling in agitated circles, like a shark with blood in the water.

After covering the dough, I take my coffee back to the couch and start the next episode of *TGBBO*. One and a half episodes later,

Heather finally opens her eyes. I'm so worked up, I blurt out, "You really think I left them heartbroken?"

Heather immediately shuts her eyes and throws the blanket over her head. Through the muffled layers, she yells, "Coffee."

I get up, taking my now empty cup and feeling like a bitch once again. My poor, actually heartbroken, hungover friend just woke up, and I immediately pounce on her with my own shit. Filling a cup for Heather, I place it on the coffee table, setting it down carefully in case she's fallen asleep under the blanket. Back in the kitchen, I make the cinnamon and sugar filling, roll out the dough, and pop the whole thing into the oven.

After refilling my own cup, I snuggle on the couch in the blankets. The room is extra cozy with the colorful lights from the Christmas tree in the corner. Heather is holding her mug of coffee with both hands, her eyes puffy and focused on the screen, which she has changed to *You've Got Mail*, our favorite of all the Meg movies.

"How are you feeling?" I ask gently.

"Terrible."

I nod. "Will cinnamon rolls help?"

Heather sighs. "No, but I will eat them."

"Do you have school today?" I ask as I set down my coffee.

Heather teaches ninth grade at the high school down the street.

She shakes her head slightly, wincing as she does. "Canceled for the snow. Lucky me, after this weekend, it's winter break."

I bring us both a plate to the couch. We spend the morning eating, sipping coffee, and watching movies. But the accusation from before that I dumped all my past boyfriends lies heavy on my heart. It nags at me so much that eventually, I make my way back to my bedroom.

Opening my thick red curtain, I let the light in, the snow still falling. Looks like the walk to work will take a bit longer today. I kneel and reach under the bed, slipping the vintage suitcase out and placing it on top of my comforter.

My breakup suitcase. Ever since I was fourteen, I've taken all the mementos I'm not ready to get rid of and shoved them into this vintage faux crocodile skin luggage. I usually don't pull it out unless there is a new batch of things to put in.

Heather comes through the door, coffee in hand. "The breakup case? I should get one of those."

I snag a Polaroid out of the side pocket as Heather sits and starts riffling through movie tickets, teddy bears, and love notes. In the picture, I'm sitting between Josh's legs, tilting my face back, and we are locked in a passionate embrace. My blonde hair looks darker in the old photo. My already fair skin is even paler, but there's a rosiness to my cheeks. I look great. Ah, the built-in filter of youth and Polaroid film.

Josh and I dated all through eleventh grade, up until the prom, when he decided to take someone else. I'm still not sure what happened there. We weren't ever exclusive, but it was a shock all the same. I definitely didn't dump *him*. Before its disastrous end, Josh and I were like peas and carrots. I show it to Heather. "Exhibit A. If anything, Josh broke up with me."

Heather takes the Polaroid. "That boy was head over heels for you, and you always had one foot out the door. You pushed him away."

She digs through the side pocket, bringing out more Polaroids. She flips one to me. It's another one of Josh and me. We're at a party. He's sitting close, looking at me intently, and I'm leaning away. She points. "This! Josh always wanted to hold your hand or be so close to you, and unless you were making out, you were always pulling away."

Is that true? I look through the stack of photos of Josh and me. In every one of them, if we're not kissing, my body is turned away from him. But we were kids. And I'm not really the most casually affectionate person.

"Hmm." I'm still examining the evidence when Heather gasps so loud, I jump back. "What? Is it a spider?"

I fucking hate spiders. Adrenaline shoots to my heart, and I scan the room for something I can use to kill it. I land on a baking magazine, quickly snatch it off my bedside table, and roll it up. I really don't want to get bug guts on it—inside, there's a recipe for a pear tart I'd really like to try—but desperate times...

I hold it up and rush to Heather's side, but there's no spider. No creepy crawly critters at all, in fact. Heather is holding a small blue velvet box. She snaps it open. Inside is a gold ring with a solitary square diamond. It's simple and elegant. On the top of the box is a little note that says in cursive, *Marry me?*

"Ruby!" Heather says. "What the fuck is this? You were engaged? Why didn't you tell me? Who gave this to you? Was it from Nick?"

I shake my head and realize I'm still holding the magazine like I'm going to whack the ring. The gorgeous ring that I have never, not once, seen in my entire life.

"I have no idea," I say, throwing the magazine on the bed. "Where did you find it?"

Heather hands the ring to me. "It was at the bottom, under some of the books."

My first thought is Grandma. Somehow, someway, this ring is her doing. Handing the ring back, I run out to the hall closet with Heather calling after me.

"Where are you going?"

I'm back a moment later with a thick, leather-bound photo album. I start flipping through the plastic pages, yellowing now with age. There's my grandmother and her sister as little girls, drawing on the wall with crayons in this very house. There's Grandma in her graduation gown. Heather points to a picture of a man on a motorcycle with a cap on instead of a helmet. He's leaned over with a cigarette hanging out of his mouth.

"Who's that?"

"No idea." I look closely. The black-and-white photo is slightly out of focus and very grainy. It could be my grandpa. I don't think he ever smoked, though. I keep flipping, because it's not what I'm looking for. A couple more pages, and I find it. A picture of my grandma and grandpa with her hand over her heart. Her engagement ring is the focal point of the picture, with an oval-shaped diamond. I know we buried her with it on her finger five years ago.

I take the ring again, holding it up to the picture. "It wasn't my grandma's. This one is square."

"Princess cut," Heather says.

I look at her. "How do you know that?"

"How do you not?"

If this ring isn't left over from the suitcase, then how did it get in there? Was one of my exes really going to propose? Who? Maybe one of them did have deeper feelings than I thought.

The clock on the nightstand switches over and, in bright-red, announces it's already noon. With all this snow, I'm going to be late.

"Shit. I have to get ready for my shift at the bar." I hand the ring back to Heather like we're playing a game of hot potato and practically run to the shower. I scrub like I can wash away the millions of questions swirling through my head—the main one being, where the hell did that ring come from? I throw on jeans and a black sweater. The snow hasn't stopped, so I put on my thickest socks and dig out my snow boots from the back of the closet.

I put on my cropped puffer coat, wishing I'd gone for the full-length one when I bought this last year on a trip to Seattle. Heather's back on the couch, ring box clutched in her hand, eyes fixed blankly on the screen.

"Honey, I have to go to work, but you're welcome to stay."

"Okay," she says without looking away from Harry meeting Sally.

I head over and wrap her in a big hug. "I love you."

"I love you, too." We part, and she looks up at me. "Which one of the boys you dumped was ready to propose, do you think?" She hands me the ring box.

"Heather. I didn't dump…" I don't know what to say. If one of my exes was going to propose, clearly their feelings ran deeper than I realized at the time. Maybe she's right. Maybe I really did dump them all. Guilt coats my stomach as I shove the box into my coat pocket and give her a kiss on top of her head. "Come by the bar later if you want."

CHAPTER 2

The air outside is an arctic slap to the face. The trees shiver in the strong wind. I walk gingerly through the inch and a half of snow, the crunch under my feet so loud it echoes down the road. The bar isn't far, though. Having to concentrate on not falling on my face is a nice distraction at the very least.

The ring is heavy in my pocket as I turn onto Main Street. My family moved to Fortune Falls when I was in elementary school to be closer to my grandma. The moment we did, it felt like walking into Stars Hollow. Brick buildings mixed with weather-worn wooden Victorian-style houses line the street. Most with colorful awnings. Extra bright today against the heavy gray clouds.

I take a slight detour, even though I'm already running late, to pass the bakery. Closed, just like I thought it would be. It used to be bustling. On Sunday's, the line would wrap around the block. Grandma, Grandpa, and I would all stand in it after church—them holding hands, me bouncing on my toes and pretending to be a balle-rina. But these days, the bakery is closed more than it's open. Rumor is the owner is going to retire and sell the business. I picture myself wearing a cute apron with daisies printed on it standing behind the counter, greeting customers, and serving them my baked goods. But I push the thought away. It's silly. I have some savings but not buy-a-bakery money.

I head back to my route. The Vern sign is lit up in the blustery sky for blocks before I reach the painted red door. It's called The Vern because the sign was smashed decades ago, just the "Vern" in Tavern surviving. It occurs to me now that I have no idea how the sign was destroyed.

The heavy red wooden door swings open with a squeak in protest from the hinges.

"Brrr." I stamp my feet on the mat.

"You wouldn't be so cold if you wore a hat," Kyle's deep voice calls out from somewhere in the back.

My hand flies to my mass of curls. It's enough of a look on its own without adding a hat. That would be a lot.

The familiar dark-wood bar, colorful Tiffany lamps, and red vinyl booths feel as warm as the air that greets me, though. Who needs a hat when you have a cozy bar? Cozy and completely empty, which is not too surprising for a Wednesday afternoon. *White Christmas*, starring Bing Crosby, Rosemary Clooney, Danny Kaye, and Vera-Ellen, plays on the television in the corner. It's the train scene—my favorite—and I pause a moment to watch.

I'm still standing there when Kyle walks out of the back completely tangled in Christmas lights. His prominent biceps are flexing, stretching his white T-shirt as he tries to unwrap the strand off his head, and his usually slicked-back black hair is mussed up. His eyes are wide. "Help."

I laugh and wish I had my Polaroid camera with me. I should really take it everywhere I go. Instead, I pull my phone out of my pocket and snap a picture. "Say cheese."

"No, this does not need to be documented." His full lips frown. He spins, but that just wraps the lights tighter.

"Hold on. Stay still." I shrug off my puffer jacket and stash it on the little shelf behind the bar.

I come over and try to find the end of the cord. My fingers roam the tangled mess, every now and then feeling the warmth of Kyle's skin. He smells like a snowy day. Woodsmoke, wool, and something unique to him. It's a little sweet but smells clean somehow. I almost lean in even closer to get a better whiff, but that would be weird. Kyle and I are friends. Good friends. Friends don't smell each other.

I motion my head in the direction of the television, where *White Christmas* is still playing. "Who washes their hair with snow?"

"Isn't that some YouTube challenge?" His deep voice is full of mirth today. It is most days. In our five years of working together, I think I've seen Kyle in a bad mood twice. Even before that, in high school, I'd never seen him really mad. Not to say he's a pushover by any means. He's sent drunk disorderly dudes out on their ear, but he always walks back in with a smile on his face. Most of the time, Kyle is a positive person. Always happy to be here, happy to greet the customers, happy to see me.

I find the end and start detangling the lights. "Was this a YouTube challenge?"

"No. I was getting them out of the box, and they fell on me. I'm a little late with the Christmas decorations this year. Usually Mitch…" His voice trails off.

I nod and keep working. We don't have to go there today.

Once I have the lights in my hand, I hand them back to Kyle.

He smiles. "Thank you."

Smiling back, I lock eyes with him. They're dark brown, with a lighter center around his pupil that shifts depending on the light. It's something I've always noticed. Right now, they're catching the hanging Tiffany lamp just right. Warm honey. "I always have your back."

There is a heavy pause where the only sound is the movie and our soft breaths. I break the moment, brushing my hands on my jeans and heading behind the bar. I grab some lemons from the plastic bin on the counter.

There's a loud bang from the kitchen.

Kyle points at the door. "Billy's in the back doing some work."

Nodding, I pick up a knife and start slicing the lemons. As my hands find a rhythm, my mind flits from one thought to the next until it gets firmly stuck…on the ring. Who could've given me that ring? And why would they give it to me and not actually propose?

The thing Heather said is still bothering me, too. Did I really hurt all those people? I was so sure there were no hard feelings, no deep feelings at all on either side.

Once a heap of lemons is sliced, I grab an order ticket and start to make a list. Kyle comes to stand next to me, pulling a beer for one of the two customers we have at the moment.

Kyle nods over to the paper. "What are you doing there?"

I sigh and look up into Kyle's face. His nose is a little crooked—not overly so, but enough that I wonder if he broke it as a kid. Maybe at one point in his life, he was a fighter. I can't picture sweet Kyle ever purposefully getting into a fight, though.

I'm momentarily lost for a minute until he says, "Ruby?"

I snap back to the present. "Do you think I'm heartless?"

He raises an eyebrow and sounds curious when he replies. "No, Ruby. You're not heartless. What makes you ask that?"

"The men I've dated…" I fiddle with the pen in my hand. "Do you think I dumped them all?"

Kyle smiles, shakes his head, and laughs. He smiles all the way across the room to hand Mr. McGregor his Pabst and the whole way back. By the time he's next to me again, he's wiping a tear away from under his eye, still trying to stifle his chuckles.

My hands fly to my hips as I simmer at his laughter. "Why is that funny?"

He takes a deep breath. "It's just…not what I expected *you* of all people to ask."

My cheeks warm, a fire burning in my belly at his words. I bend, snagging a rag from the bucket, and wipe the already clean bar for something to do with my hands as I ask, "What does that mean, me of all people?"

Kyle turns to look at me, really look at me. The joy is gone from his face. "I didn't realize you were serious. I wouldn't have laughed…" He pauses. "How do I put this… You have to agree you're in a rela-tionship to dump someone, right? And you don't do relationships.

You don't seem to have much interest in romance at all. At least not since Nick, and even then, you said it was just fun."

The mention of Nick makes my shoulders tense. "What makes you say that? You know about Margs and Meg Tuesday. Those movies are mostly romances. And if I ever get ahold of the remote in this place, I usually put on a rom-com."

Kyle frowns. "That's movies, though. Whenever a guy tries to flirt or ask you out, you shut them down so fast, they don't know what hit 'em."

Is that really how he sees me? "That's not true."

But as my mind clicks through time after time of customers trying to chat me up, I realize maybe it is. But I'm working. I'm not supposed to flirt with customers.

Kyle lowers his voice and steps in closer, so close I can smell his minty fresh breath. "What about Billy? He's asked you out like five times, and you always say no."

I let out a long, slow breath and whisper right back, "I don't want to date Billy."

Kyle shrugs. "That's what I'm saying. You don't want to date anyone. Your whole no-relationship rule."

That's true.

I check the time. Shit. It's getting late, and I still need to go to the bank. I head to the back and into the office to the safe to get last night's deposit. I hurry out so Billy doesn't catch me and try to ask me out a sixth time.

As I put on my coat, Kyle runs a hand through his hair. "Hey, you're not pissed, are you? You caught me off guard, is all."

"Not pissed. Bank closes early today. See you in a minute."

It's still snowing as I head outside. Good thing the bank is only a couple of blocks away. I wish I didn't have to walk so slowly so I don't fall on my ass. I'd like to power walk, get my blood pumping, work off some of this swirling anger. It's silly to be so mad. I just didn't know that's how Kyle saw me, as someone not interested in dating. How everyone sees me, apparently. I'm not even sure why it bothers me so much, besides the fact that it's absolutely not true.

I walk past the tattoo parlor and spy Josh inside, bent over someone's arm, tattoo gun in hand. Josh from the Polaroid. My boyfriend from October of tenth grade to spring, right before prom. This is not my first time seeing him. He comes into The Vern all the time. His trivia team usually gets third or fourth, depending on how many beers they've all had and whether or not those beers had whiskey backs. For some reason, though, after looking at those photos and finding the ring, today feels different. The hurt feels fresh. The bruise I thought was long ago healed has been poked.

At the time, he made it all seem so casual, so normal that he would take someone else to prom, that I played along. Pretended it didn't bother me, that I had no interest in school dances, anyway. We were still friends. Suddenly we were friends that didn't kiss or hold hands. Then he dropped off the random stuff I left at his house—my DVD copy of *Addicted to Love* and a bracelet, among other things. Could the ring have been in with all that other stuff?

A fierce wind blows. I wrap my arms around my torso, trying to keep the heat in.

The bank is even more empty and, if possible, even more beige than usual today. The tan tile is gleaming in the overhead lights. Maureen is reading a book, her arms propped up on the solid oak counter.

I clutch the deposit bag and walk up to the counter, my snow boots thumping on the pristine tile.

"Hey there, Ruby. How's your Monday?" Maureen sets her book down and gives me a bright smile.

"Pretty good," I say as I slide the bag across the counter.

As Maureen grabs the bag and unzips it, I dig through my pockets for the change order. I pull the ring out and place it on the counter, retrieving the scrap of paper that had fallen deep into my pocket.

Maureen throws down the money she was counting. "Girl, what is this?" She picks up the box and snaps it open. Adjusting her glasses down on her nose, she peers at the stone like a jeweler inspecting a new piece.

"Yeah, I'm not entirely sure." I fumble, watching her turn the ring this way and that, the diamond sparkling in the light.

"This is a nice ring. Simple, elegant. It's to the point." She places the ring box on the counter and picks back up the money. "Whoever gave you that, I'd say yes."

The one thing Maureen loves more than telling a story is giving advice.

"No, it's not…"

But Maureen keeps talking, counting as she does. "Artie and I were married for twenty-one years before he passed. When I was your age—well, maybe a bit younger…"

Looks like I'm getting both advice and a story today. But I can understand the need to talk about people you miss, so I lean in and nod.

"My parents were all about a long engagement. And I listened. I made Artie wait a whole year. He's been gone twelve years now, and I wish with all my heart I could've had that extra time as his wife."

"It's not like that," I try to explain.

Maureen puts the deposit slip in the bag along with the change. She slides it across the counter and then takes my hands in hers. Her palm is soft but cold. "Ruby, don't wait. Our time here is not guaranteed. If you love the owner of that ring, you need to jump headfirst. Take the plunge. Say yes!"

She snatches the ring and slides it on my finger, her smile so bright the ring twinkles in it. She squeezes my hand. I squeeze hers back, swallowing hard and fighting against the sudden prickle in the back of my eyes. I know more than most that our time here is limited.

"Thanks, Maureen." I put the ring box back into my pocket, grab the money bag, and head out into the cold.

CHAPTER 3

When I get back to The Vern, Heather is sitting at the bar, her long red hair cascading down her back, her oversize black sweater pulled down over her hands cupping a mug. I come up behind her and give her an enormous hug.

She squeals. "Ick, your coat is wet. And you're freezing."

I head behind the bar, scooting past Kyle. He moves instinctively to let me by. We've moved together behind this tight bar so many times, it's like an unconscious dance at this point.

As I take off my coat, Kyle's brow furrows. "Did you get engaged on the way to the bank?"

Heather sits straighter. "Oh my God. You're wearing the ring now?"

I sigh. "No, it…" I think of how to explain Maureen at the bank, but really, there's no way to explain her. So I just say, "Maureen."

Kyle pauses, frozen in his spot. "You asked Maureen, from the bank, to marry you? Talk about a May-December romance."

I swat him on the arm.

He makes an exaggerated flinch. "What? I'm not ageist. I'm just surprised."

"I did not ask anyone to marry me on the way to the bank. Okay?"

I wipe down a glass that is both sparkling clean and completely dry to hide my flushed cheeks.

Heather sits up straighter, color coming into her cheeks. "We found this ring in Ruby's breakup suitcase."

"Wait." Kyle's normally smiling lips pull into a tight frown. "You have a breakup suitcase?"

I shrug, but before I can say anything, Heather jumps in again. "That's not the point. She has this engagement ring, right? And absolutely no idea who it's from."

A curl falls into my face, and I wish, not for the first time, I had manageable straight hair like Heather instead of this mass of frizzy ringlets with a mind of its own. I take the hair tie off my wrist and pull it all up and out of my face.

Kyle nods. "So one of your exes was going to propose, but you dumped them first and they gave you the ring without you realizing?"

"I did not dump them. This is what I've been saying. It was casual. They knew it. I knew it. No hard feelings."

Heather frowns into her mug and shakes her head. "You've dumped all of them, Ruby."

"No, I haven't."

Kyle looks away quickly, but he's nodding along with Heather.

There's a large crash in the back. Kyle frowns as he puts a hand softly on my shoulder while moving past me. Heather raises her eyebrows.

His hand falls away as he keeps moving toward the back. "I'll go check on Billy."

Heather looks at me, her whole face a lecture.

"What?" I say.

"You need to put a baby in that gorgeous man."

"That's not how that works at all." A laugh escapes me. "Anyway, it's not like that between us."

It's not. I've known Kyle since we were in a high school production of *Sweeney Todd*. He was a senior, I was a sophomore, and we were both terrible. So, we were strongly encouraged to hang near the back. He got me this job. Introduced me to Mitch. If Heather had suggested back in high school that he liked me, I would've died. But now we're good friends, and that's all.

"I have enough problems." I dig my list out of my jeans pocket and smooth it out.

Heather peers over the bar. "What you got there?"

"It's my love-life list. It's the possible people the ring could've been from." And it's a lot shorter than I expected.

Heather snatches the list, nodding.

A couple walks in and sits down. I go over and take their order of a whiskey and a beer.

When I come back to Heather, she's making notes on the list. "We need to talk to them. All of them. Give me your phone."

"My phone?"

"Yes. I'm going to text Liam."

"Liam? No. I can't just message him. No, no, no."

"Where is he living?"

I blow out my cheeks. We're still Facebook friends, so I see his posts every now and then. "I think he's in Beachside."

"That's not far at all. Do you know where he works?" Heather's eyes have lost that dull, lifeless quality that settled in after she told me what happened last night.

I nod. "I do. But we can't show up there out of the blue. Plus, I have to work all week."

Kyle comes out from the back with Billy close behind. Billy tries to catch my eye, but I quickly look away. Kyle gives him a slap on the back. "Thanks, man. You have the key, yeah?"

"Yep. We'll start work tomorrow."

"Sounds good."

Kyle comes back behind the bar and stands right next to me. He hangs his head in his hands, his elbows resting on the counter, his forearms flexing under the weight. I put a hand on his back. The strong muscles underneath his T-shirt are hard and warm under my palm.

"What is it?"

"We have to close."

"What?"

He takes a deep breath that I can feel under my palm and stands, clearing his throat. "Folks, drinks are on us, but I'm sorry, The Vern is closed. Everyone needs to leave. We have a minor emergency."

The four customers in the place don't put up a fight as they head out the door. Heather starts to stand as well, but I motion for her to stay.

Once everyone else is gone, I say, "Kyle, what is going on?"

"When Billy moved the old range to replace it, a chunk of wall came with it, and he found black mold. A lot of it. They're going to have to rip it all out and build us some new walls." Kyle grabs a bottle of whiskey and three shot glasses, pouring us each a double.

"Shit." I take the glass from him, our fingers brushing slightly.

"Billy says it should take two weeks, maybe three. Best-case scenario, we can open for New Year's."

"Shit," I say again. There go my holiday tips.

Heather throws back her shot and wipes her mouth, standing from the stool. "This is perfect!"

Both Kyle and I look at her, mouths agape.

She keeps going. "Now we can track down the people on your list and find out who the ring was from. We don't have to text or DM. We can go speak to them all in person, just like you want."

God, is that what I want?

"One of them isn't too far, but the other is way up in the mountains in Washington, last I heard. Plus, I don't drive, and you don't have a car."

"I can borrow my brother's van," Heather retorts. "Come on. It'll be fun!"

Nerves crackle in my chest. "I don't know."

"Let's go make a pizza and figure it out."

I nod and look at Kyle. "Want to come over for pizza?"

He smiles, grabbing his coat. "I love pizza."

I throw the rest of the shot down my throat and slam the glass onto the counter, feeling the burn travel down my throat. "Let's go."

WE ALL PILE into Kyle's truck and head to my place. His truck is nice, cherry red and roomy, not at all like my grandpa's old beater was.

As soon as we walk through the door, I kick off my snow boots. Kyle is the last one in and shuts it behind him. We all shrug off our heavy coats and place them on the bench in the entryway.

Even though it's only a little past six, it's dark outside—like *middle of the night* dark. I head right for the kitchen. If we're going to make a plan, we need food. Heather comes in and takes a seat at the kitchen table. Kyle comes through the doorway and freezes.

"Mmmm." He leans dramatically against the doorframe, his white T-shirt shifting, showing the slightest hint of skin above his belt. "What is that heavenly smell?"

Heather smiles. "Ruby made cinnamon rolls from scratch."

Kyle nods as he takes a seat at the table. "I knew you liked to bake, but cinnamon rolls are next level."

Heat warms my cheeks at the admiration in his voice...and possibly at the sliver of skin I spied. I've always had a little crush on Kyle, but I don't usually ogle him this much. It must be the love-life list getting under my skin, and my mind—or hormones—is searching for a distraction. I pull a frozen pizza out of the freezer and pop it into the oven. Then I bring a bottle of red to the table with three jelly jars. Kyle gets to work opening the wine, while I pull the list out of my pocket and smooth it onto the table.

"Only three people," Heather says as she examines the list. "Easy peasy."

I read over the names and don't quite feel the easy peasiness of it. Two of these people I haven't talked to in years. And I'm pretty sure they would be happy if they never spoke to me again.

"And," Heather adds, "you can talk to Josh before we leave."

Kyle hands us each a glass of the Cabernet.

Heather has her phone out now and is tapping away. "Do you have a map?"

"Uh…" I mentally dig through my stuff, clearly picturing a box in the second bedroom. "I think I have an old cycling map somewhere."

She swallows a heavy swig from her jar and holds up her pointer finger. "Get it. We need to mark where everyone is."

"There's not that many, we could just use our phones—"

Heather waves my suggestion away.

Kyle smirks and says, "Need help?"

"Sure."

We walk down the hall, Kyle following close behind me. We walk right past the master bedroom with the open door. My grandmother's bed is still made. Her sewing table's in the corner. The timer is still set, so the lamp is on, and it's all illuminated in a soft amber glow. It warms my heart and squeezes it all at the same time.

I head into my room and open the closet as Kyle moves around the space. He's been to my house hundreds of times over the years, but we always stay in the living room, usually watching some cheesy nineties movie he brought over.

"This room's a lot smaller than the other one," he says as he sizes up the space.

I shrug. "Is it?"

I know it is. I'm well aware. When I was around sixteen, my mom accepted the position of head fitness instructor on a cruise ship. I moved in with my grandma. I was relentless in trying to convince her I needed the larger room. It has a full-length mirror. I could get ready for school so much faster with the en suite bathroom. My growing limbs need the space, I told her, at which point I would lie down like a starfish, wherever we were—on the couch, in the car, on the floor of the kitchen… She would howl with laughter.

I was teasing. I'd never oust her out of her own room. But it made her laugh. I loved that sound. My chest tightens at the memory, and I bite my lip.

"I like the view from this room." I point out the window, which looks out at the extremely plain backyard, now covered in snow.

Kyle nods, but the look in his eyes tells me he's not buying it.

"So…" He claps his hands together, his smile lighting up the room more than my lamp in the corner. "A mysterious ring from an unknown origin. Sounds like an epic quest."

I laugh. "I don't know about epic, Frodo. We at least know it's from one of the three people on the list."

Kyle nods. "If you had to put money on one, which would it be?"

Mentally, I scan the list, the faces of my exes scrolling through my mind. It's a real mystery. "Honestly, I have absolutely no idea."

I reach up to grab the box, but it's heavier than I remember, and I start tipping backward. Kyle jumps into action, stepping behind me, his body hot on my back, his arm near my face as he reaches for the box, steadying it. We stay there for a long moment. I'm not sure how to move without the box going into my face.

"Whoa. I got it." He moves his other hand, and I'm engulfed in his scent. I close my eyes and feel the weight lift out of my hands.

My back is instantly cold as Kyle steps back and places the box on the bed.

"Thanks," I say as I open the box and grab the map. "Here it is."

I head to the kitchen, my cheeks flushed, and spread out the map on the table. Taking my wine, I check on the pizza.

Kyle comes back into the room, brushing his hands off on his jeans. "What's the plan? Hmm, that smells good."

I pull the pizza out, cut it, and bring it over to the table.

Heather's been busy. There are two stars marked on the map, each with a name scrawled underneath it.

Kyle inspects each location. "Two? I thought we were hunting down three exes..."

I swat him on the arm. "We are not hunting them down."

He shrugs, taking a huge mouthful of pizza.

Heather caps the Sharpie. "The last one is right here in town."

Taking a sip of my wine, I look over the map.

Heather points to the star about ninety miles away. "We start here with Liam."

An uneasiness settles in my stomach. This is not a good idea. I should put the ring back in the breakup case and forget all about this. I frown. "I don't know."

Heather stares pointedly at the ring on my finger I still haven't taken off and looks up at me with puppy dog eyes.

A heavy sigh escapes me. "Fine."

I guess we're doing this. Heather's smiling from ear to ear. At the very least, raking over my past is cheering her up and making her forget about her own problems. The faces of the men on the list come to mind. I really hope I didn't leave them heartbroken, like Heather thinks. I take a large slug of wine. No better time to find out and, if I did, apologize at the very least. What could go wrong?

CHAPTER 4

Heather and I start making a more solid plan of which town we'll go to first.

Kyle gets up from the table, slapping his hands on his jeans. "Well, I should go. You ladies need to get some sleep if you're leaving first thing in the morning. And I have a lot to get done while the bar is closed. Gotta go get my ducks in a row."

"Ah, come on. Let them meander," I say with a smile as I walk him to the door. I don't want him to leave. It's late and cold. "You could stay. You've been drinking."

He tugs on a rogue curl that has escaped my messy bun. "I had half a glass with the pizza." He shrugs on his coat, points to the living room and then to me. "You two have been *drinking*."

I wave him away, but he's not wrong. The wine was delicious, the company friendly as the snow steadily fell outside. I've had a couple of glasses. Heather, well, she's still wiping away the memory of her ex-boyfriend's blow job.

"You sure you want to go tomorrow? You two could think about it for a couple days. Bar's closed two full weeks, at least. Plenty of time."

Heather yells from the kitchen, "We can't lose momentum!"

I smile. "Hard to argue with that."

"So away you go."

He wraps his scarf around his neck. The fabric looks so soft, I reach out to touch the end. Kyle smirks, his brow furrowing as he does. He yanks the scarf back and throws it dramatically over his shoulder.

We both dissolve into laughter.

"Okay," Kyle says once we've composed ourselves. "Let me know if you need anything. I can drive out to wherever, whenever."

My heart feels fuller than my belly full of pizza at the offer. He is always there for me. "Don't worry. We got this."

WE PLANNED on leaving at eight, nine at the latest. But as I wake up to gray winter light trickling through the opening in my curtains, I can feel it's much, much later. I check my phone.

Shit.

Ten o'clock and three missed calls. I bolt out of bed, running to the couch where I left Heather last night. After Kyle took off, we hooked up the VCR, dusted off my copy of *French Kiss*, and snuggled back into the blanket nest. Heather fell asleep right before Meg Ryan caught her fiancé kissing another woman. Thank God. I'd forgotten about that whole storyline. I'd tucked her in, washed my face like the responsible adult I am, and gone to bed. My room had still smelled the faintest bit of Kyle. But it wasn't just my room. It was on my pillow. I'd inhaled deeply, put on the ring, and twisted it on my finger as I'd drifted to sleep, wondering who it was from.

But now, as we're two hours behind her carefully written plan, Heather is nowhere to be found.

Without thinking, I dial her number. No answer. I check my voicemail, and I have one from her.

"Ruby, it's me. Hey, so Theo called last night after you went to bed. We talked for hours. He's really turned a corner." She lowers her voice. "He's even made an appointment with a therapist. Anyway, he picked me up this morning, and we're going away for the holidays.

Don't hate me. You should still go track down your exes. It'll be good for you. I went ahead and reserved rooms for the nights we talked about. I sent you an email with all the reservation details. Love you."

Love you. Love you, but abandoned you after I came up with this totally unhinged plan to excavate your love life.

Shit. *Heather.* How can she want to go back to that asshole after what he did? I've never liked him. He always gave me the ick. This is the first time she caught him, but I highly doubt this is the first time he's cheated on her. Your first time is not in the parking lot of Mariners Market. Now, your thirtieth time might be.

I let out a deep breath and plop onto the couch, covering myself in the blanket. This is actually a good thing. Besides the Heather going back to Theo part. Now, I can put the ring back in the box and not have to worry at all about it. Go about my day. Only with no work.

Clicking on *Home Alone,* I try to snuggle into the blankets, but I can't sit still. I wander to the kitchen. My happy place. The light wafting through the lemon-yellow curtains instantly lifts my mood. The ring, however, is practically burning the skin on my finger, so I take it off by the kitchen sink. I wash my hands and get to work. First, I make a sugar cookie recipe that was Grandma's favorite. We made it for almost every holiday. Hearts for Valentine's, eggs for Easter, leaves for the first day of fall. Today, it's finally time to make the Christmas cookies.

While the dough is chilling, I use the time to make a quick batch of no bakes. A favorite of my mom's. Before her whole *no sugar* kick, anyway. As I stir the chocolate on the stove, the ring catches my eye. The ring. *The fucking ring.*

Who could've given it to me, and why didn't I know? Once the plan was made, I started to feel almost excited last night. I thought maybe it was seeing Heather happy. But I think I really do want to know who this is from and what happened.

I roll out the dough and press out stars, reindeer, and gingerbread men over and over. I bake for two hours, all the while thinking about the ring. By the time the last batch is out of the oven, I've worked myself into a frenzy. Sliding the ring back onto my finger, I click off the oven. Then I get dressed in record time, throw on my coat, and head out the door.

Each step as I trudge through the snow solidifies my resolve. This ring had to come from someone, and I am going to find out who. Not for Heather, not to cheer her up, but for my own peace of mind.

The tattoo shop is relatively empty when I get there. One customer near the back is getting work done on her forearm. "Fairytale of New York" plays softly. And no Josh. My shoulders slump. I'm about to turn to leave when Josh strolls out of the back with an armful of empty bottles. He sees me standing near the door and smiles.

"Ruby." He sets down the bottles and comes over to stand behind the counter. "Finally going to get that tat?"

When I was younger, we talked a lot about tattoos, including what we would get once we were old enough. I always wanted to get a hummingbird. They were my grandma's favorite. So many times, I sat at the kitchen table stirring cake batter or rolling out dough, when we would both stop to admire a hummingbird at the feeder right outside the window. But when I turned eighteen, I was too busy taking her to appointments to think about it. When she passed... Well, I haven't been ready.

"No." I lay both hands on the glass counter, the ring sparkling in the light. Josh hardly even glances at it as he pulls the stool behind him closer and takes a seat.

"What can I do for you, then?"

I drum my fingers as he fiddles with some papers. Josh doesn't take his eyes off the sheets of flash tattoos.

It occurs to me that we are both adults, and our "relationship" was over years ago. I can come right out and ask him.

"Josh, did I dump you?"

He freezes mid-flick, a drawing of an eagle in his hand. For a second, I think I may have broken him, but he sets the papers down after a beat, blinking several times. "What are you talking about?"

"Eleventh grade. You and I were hanging out. Then you took Jane to the prom. Did I dump you before that?"

"You didn't dump me." Josh shakes his head. "*You* didn't want to be my girlfriend—like, at all."

What is he talking about? My mind flashes back to seeing Jane and him together in the halls at school, the sting. "That's crazy."

"Um, no, it's not." Josh folds his arms across his chest. "We went out for milkshakes at Stonehouse, and we saw an old couple celebrating something, remember?"

A vague memory comes back to me of the day he's talking about. Our knees knocking under the table, the cold sweetness on my tongue from the milkshake, the dread sitting in my stomach like a pit... because while I was there, Grandma was home recovering from another round of chemo. "Kind of."

"I said they were probably celebrating their anniversary, and that might be us someday. I was about to ask you to be my girlfriend, when you pulled your hand away and said that would never be us."

I remember now. I'd said that was a silly fantasy. Those two had lived in denial their whole life together. That what they had would end someday, just like everything else. It was better to keep things light. Not take life so seriously.

Josh recites the last thing I said before I got up and walked to the door, leaving my unfinished milkshake and him. "'Relationships are dumb,' I think were your exact words."

He pulls over the binder on the counter and starts slipping the drawings into the plastic sleeves.

"Right, I do remember all that," I say.

"I tried calling you later that day to talk about it, but you wouldn't call me back. So, I figured that was your way of showing me the door, so to speak."

I can feel it from his side of the table, how much that would've hurt. "It wasn't my intention, but I can see how it looked that way, yeah."

"Anyway, it all worked out for the best," Josh says, flipping the binder shut. "Janey and I are talking about marriage."

I smile, an honest, real smile. Josh was always a good guy, and I genuinely am glad he's happy. "That's wonderful. Congratulations."

I'm about to turn and walk back home, but the ring feels heavy on my finger. I have to ask. I swallow hard, not sure how to put this. So, instead of being delicate, I hold up my finger and blurt out, "Were you going to propose…to me, I mean?"

"Propose?" Josh laughs. "Ruby, we were seventeen. No, I was going to ask if you wanted to go steady."

"With a ring?" I say, waving my fingers.

Josh holds it out to examine it. "No. I've never seen this before. It's pretty, though."

I nod. "Thanks, Josh, and congratulations again."

The air outside is still bitterly cold, the snow falling in light tufts. While I'm no closer to figuring out where this ring came from, I actually feel better. I feel good. All this time, I'd thought Josh had lost interest, when really, he'd thought I didn't want to be with him. Then he started dating the love of his life. It was meant to be. It was beyond me. If all this hadn't happened the way it did, they wouldn't be about to get married.

This is great. This is why people go on and on about needing closure. It feels amazing. Like hopping into a hot shower after being out in this snow.

I need to talk to the other two guys on my list.

Digging my phone out of my pocket, I call Kyle, and he picks up on the first ring. "Hey, are you busy?"

"Define busy," he says through what sounds like a mouthful of cereal.

"The thing is… You know how you offered to drive on this road trip…"

"To hunt down your exes?"

"We are not *hunting.* I just want to talk to them."

He laughs. "Semantics."

"I want to see if they remember things the same way and if maybe the ring is from one of them. And if I need to apologize, I will. I think I need closure."

"As long as it's cool that we end up in Leavenworth before

Christmas Eve, I can drive." His voice is soft, all the teasing having gone out of it.

"Works for me. Are you sure you can go? I know—"

Kyle's voice is clear, no feral munching as he says, "If you need me, I'm there. Give me twenty minutes."

CHAPTER 5

I rush back home, as much as one can rush in what is now mushy ice on the streets. Once I'm through the door, I turn on my shower to warm up the old pipes. Kyle will be here soon, and I need to shower before he gets here.

Throwing off my coat, I'm about to set my phone down when I see a missed text from Heather.

Heather: Call me.

I hit the little FaceTime button in the corner.

Her face pops up after a moment. She says in a low voice, "I said call."

I hiss right back, "I did."

She moves the phone, and the screen is muffled gray.

"I'm going to step outside for a bit," I hear her yell. Her face comes on the screen again.

There's the sound of the wind.

"There, that's better. Do you hate me?" she asks, wrinkling her brow.

"Yes."

"Come on. Theo's really turned things around."

I bite my lip to stop myself from saying I'm sure he's turned someone around.

"Ruby, I love him."

Love. I will myself not to roll my eyes. Love sounds awful. Being completely blind to who the other person actually is—which in Theo's case is a cheater and a liar and a general piece of shit.

Heather's eyes are watering. "I really didn't mean to leave you hanging. If you need me, I'll head back right now."

I try to smile. "No, it's fine. Kyle's on the way over, and we're going to Beachside."

Heather puts a hand to her heart. "Wonderful. I emailed. Did you get it?"

I haven't had time this morning to check my email, but I nod. "Yep, all set."

She smiles wide, her eyes light. "Yay. Text me all the details."

"I will. Heather, be careful, okay?"

"Me? You're the one about to go on an epic adventure with a very handsome man."

As I shake my head, heat rises to my cheeks. Steam is billowing out of the bathroom. Shit, the shower. I head to my bedroom. "Heather, I have to go."

"Me too. Love you."

I blow a kiss and click off. How can she be so naïve? I take off my pants, getting ready for the shower. How can she think Theo is not going to cheat on her again? It's stupid, and Heather is not stupid. I wriggle out of my shirt and throw it onto my bed.

Fucking *love.* Love has blinded her. It's somehow nullified her common sense. He's going to break her heart, and I'm going to have to carefully stitch it back together. Then I'm going to stab him with the sewing needle.

There's a knock at the door. I stomp my way through the living room. I'm so pissed off and panicked, I fling open the front door without a second thought.

The blast of cold air on my massive amount of exposed skin is my first sign, and Kyle's shocked face is my second, that I should really think before I act. Goosebumps cover my flesh as I stand in the doorway in nothing but my underwear.

This day keeps getting better and better.

I slam the door in Kyle's face.

"Sorry," I yell through the solid plank of wood. I go to grab a coat, but my cropped puffer doesn't really do a lot to help the *no pants* situation.

"Ruby, are you okay?" Kyle asks, his voice full of genuine concern. "We said twenty minutes, right?"

We sure did. I look around, picking up a scarf and trying to wrap it around my waist.

"Should I come back?"

How many times have we been swimming together at the lake? This is no different. Sometimes we've gone on a whim and both jumped into the water in our underwear. Plus, it's Kyle. It's totally fine. I throw the scarf down, wrap the puffer coat closer around my torso, and open the door.

Kyle's holding a tray of paper cups, and the smell is heavenly. His eyes move over my face and keep moving down, past the puffer jacket to my bare legs. Once he gets there, his eyes snap back to mine, the tips of his ears pink.

"I was just hopping into the shower," I say and move to let Kyle come in.

He nods and hands me one of the cups. "Mocha with extra whipped cream."

I take a large sip as he steps inside. Shutting the door, I feel instantly warmer. For a brief moment, I think about taking off the jacket and hanging it back on the coat rack, but I decide to take it with me to the bathroom.

Once I'm showered and dressed, I head out to the living room, still sipping on my delicious coffee. Kyle's made himself at home. He's on the couch, coffee in hand, watching sports highlights.

"I feel a bit more human now," I say, taking a seat. "Sorry about slamming the door in your face."

"Nah, not your fault. I'm the one who showed up at the exact agreed upon time for this completely unhinged adventure. Why wouldn't you slam the door in my face?"

I throw the gingerbread man decorative pillow at him. "I said sorry. I'm having a morning."

Kyle's smile falls, and his face turns into an expression of genuine concern. "Heather went back to what's his nuts."

I frown and cross my arms. "Theo."

"Ahhh." Kyle shifts, draping his arm across the couch and turning more toward me, less toward the sports on the screen. "And this is not a good thing."

"It is not. But it's also her life, so…"

Kyle nods. "It's hard to watch people you love choose to get hurt."

I sit up. That's it exactly. "Yes."

"But you can't really say anything. She won't listen. And if she and Theo are together for a while, she'll resent you."

"Yes."

"I've been there." He sinks back into the couch. "That sucks."

I sigh, settling back into the cushions, too, and wonder who he's talking about. "It does."

"Are you sure you still want to hunt down your exes?" He takes a large sip from his coffee.

I throw the decorative gingerbread girl pillow at him, and he expertly swats it away. I'm running out of decorative pillows. "We aren't hunting them down. We're just paying them a visit."

He smiles. "Like the ghosts of Christmas past."

"Exactly, but not so menacing. And not so dead." I set down my mocha. This is crazy. A whole road trip in the middle of winter to track down some people who most likely don't want to see me. We should scrap the whole idea.

But then I remember the deep peace that settled in my bones after talking to Josh. Maybe that's why people seek closure—for that feeling. The ring twinkles on my finger. I have to know who it's from. "I have to go."

Kyle clicks off the television and stands. "Let's hit it. We're burning daylight."

"You're sure you can go the whole time? Don't you have mallards to queue?" I say with a smile.

Kyle returns my smile with a little chuckle. "They're wanderers, that's for sure. But I was headed up to Leavenworth at the end of the week, anyway, so it's no problem."

"What about your real estate stuff?" When Kyle's not working at the bar, which lately has been never, he sells real estate, or as he likes to say, he deals in dreams. Selling memories before they happen.

He frowns. "No listings at the moment. I haven't had time, really, since Mitch passed."

Mitch owned The Vern forever. It was passed down in his family for generations. He lived a long, long happy life. None of us were surprised when he passed in June at the ripe old age of ninety-three. What was surprising was that he left the bar and his house to Kyle. I know he had a son, but maybe he never wanted to be part of the family business. I know he lives somewhere far away. So, I guess it's not that shocking, but Kyle certainly seemed surprised.

I don't want to rub salt in the wound. It's been a hard adjustment for Kyle going from part-time bartender to more than full-time bar owner. And now with this black mold situation… If he says he can go, I will trust he knows what he's doing.

Kyle's chestnut eyes crinkle at the corners as he says, "What else am I going to do?"

I throw the last of my mocha down my throat and slam the paper cup on the end table, feeling the sugar trickle all the way down to my toes. "Fuck it. Let's go on an adventure."

THE ROADS ARE neither the best nor the worst as we head out of Fortune Falls onto the highway headed toward Beachside. The truck is warm, my seat heater cranked to the max, Taylor Swift plays over the speakers, and the open road stretches in front of us. After about twenty minutes, when we lose radio signal, Kyle hands me his phone.

"You can play whatever's downloaded on Spotify," he says without taking his eyes off the road.

I push the phone back in his direction. "It's locked."

"Twelve nineteen."

I freeze, phone in the air, stunned. "Is that your passcode?"

"Yeah."

As I punch the numbers in, I ask, "Why have it password protected if you give the code out willy-nilly?"

He smiles, eyes flicking to me. "I don't give it out willy-nilly. I don't have anything to hide from you."

This hits me right in the chest and tingles sweeter than the sugary mocha high. I scroll through the downloaded albums, considering this. It feels nice. He trusts me. And I trust him. Just like good friends do. I'm distracted in my line of thought as I scroll from one album to the next, noticing a theme.

"Kyle."

"Ruby."

"These are all movie soundtracks."

"Nah, not all of them."

I scroll past *Eternal Sunshine of the Spotless Mind*, *Marie Antoinette*, and *Casino*. "Um, yes. All of them."

"Pretty sure if you keep scrolling, there's some Mountain Goats."

Selecting *The Royal Tenenbaums*, I set the phone on the console between us. "We have to talk about this."

"What's to talk about?" Kyle passes a very slow truck with a massive horse trailer, and my heart rate kicks up. My hand goes instinctively to the dash. Kyle is a very safe driver, but I'm not the best passenger. I'm nervous. I look out the window as we pass, and I swear, the horse and I lock eyes.

Once we're back on our side of the road, Kyle puts a warm hand on my leg. "It's okay. I'm not going to let anything happen."

I take a deep breath and let my hand drop. "I know. You're a good driver. It's not that. It's just…sometimes, things happen out of our control."

Kyle blows out a large breath, moving his hand back to the wheel. My leg feels cold and suddenly too light in its absence. Like I could float away.

He nods. "I know all about that."

Kyle lost his mom a few years before we met. We haven't talked about it a lot, but he shared bits and pieces here and there.

"Your mom."

"My mom." He glances at me and smiles, soft and warm like always, but a little sad. "You would've liked her. Well, that's not saying much—everyone liked her. But I think you two would've really gotten along."

I smile and watch Kyle as he moves his gaze back to the road. His smile is gone, and there is a far-off look in his eyes. Like he's here but not here. "What makes you think that?"

"You're both funny. Oh man, my mom had jokes for days. Always a quip back. She could have the whole room in tears."

There's a long pause. I don't rush to fill it. I know first-hand that sometimes we need silence. The space to remember.

The song changes, and Kyle turns it up. "This right here is a great song."

Nico fills the car, singing about these days. I look out the window, watching the ocean waves beyond whiz by, and think of how much my Grandma would absolutely hate this trip. She loved her home and Fortune Falls. She'd often say, *Why do we need to go anywhere when all we need is right here?* She never understood my mom's wanderlust. I have a hard time with it myself, but sitting in this warm truck, listening to music, and watching the world rush by, I can see the appeal.

CHAPTER 6

I must have fallen asleep, because I'm roused by a soft whisper. The breath is hot on the shell of my ear. Instinctively, I want to lean into the feeling. "Mmm."

"We're here."

I open my eyes and find I'm in Kyle's truck, leaning against the window, my coat covering me like a blanket. We're parked at a gas station.

Kyle moves back to his seat. "I wasn't sure where exactly we're headed in town."

I rub my eyes, trying to wake up a bit more. "Right. Right." I pull out my phone to open Heather's email. But there's absolutely no service. The email won't load. The little circle keeps spinning with no words appearing on the screen. Shit. "I don't know."

Kyle's eyebrows furrow, and his mouth purses like he sucked a lemon. It's a ridiculous expression. Despite feeling terrible for really fucking this up, I giggle.

He shakes his head. "This is not funny."

"No." I laugh harder now. "It's your face."

"Ruby. We drive all the way out here, in the snow no less, you have no idea where we're going, and now you're making fun of my face?"

"No, not like that. You're very handsome. It's..." I try to furrow my brows like his and scowl, but he's just staring at me.

"You think I'm handsome?"

I focus on my phone. I can fix this. "Come on, you know you're handsome."

He smiles and grabs his coat from the back. "I know some people think so." His large fingers work the buttons swiftly, the smile still wide on his face. "I didn't know you were one of those people. I'm going in. Want anything?"

"Nah, I'm good." I scroll to the Wi-Fi section to see if there's any network I can sign into.

He shuts the door.

The plan was to surprise Liam at work, so I need to find out where that is. There's a Wi-Fi network called "Santa's helper" and another one called "Pretty Fly for a Wifi," but both are password protected.

Shit.

I climb out of the truck to get the blood moving in my legs and stretch. The cold air feels refreshing after the drive. There's no snow on the roads here, but it feels a good ten degrees colder. I walk to the sidewalk and look down the street. Beachside's main street is filled with mostly brick buildings, the brick so worn in places that it's more white than red. Christmas lights line each one, lit up in the waning sun. It's cute, but it's got nothing on Fortune Falls.

For one, despite the fact that it's only around four p.m. right now, most of the windows on the street are dark. But there must be a café open, or maybe a bar. Every town, no matter how tiny, has a bar.

Kyle strides out of the little gas station with a bottle of water in each hand. He spots me standing on the sidewalk and gives me a smile. Kyle is a great smiler. When he smiles, his eyes crinkle softly at the corners and his teeth gleam. It lights up his whole face, but it feels like the light is coming from within rather than shining on him.

I smile, but my stomach twists uncomfortably. How am I going to tell him that I don't know where the hell we're supposed to go in this town? We both hop back into the truck. Kyle turns it on, cranking the heater. I rub my hands, placing them in front of one of the vents while Kyle buckles his seat belt.

"Where to, Captain?"

Where to? The clock in the center console catches my eye. Four seventeen. We can check into the hotel. They'll have Wi-Fi. Then I can write down the plan so this kind of thing won't happen again. The hotel is saved in my map searches at least. "I think we should check in and freshen up. We can figure out our next step there."

"You got it. Just tell me where I'm headed."

As we drive down the main road in this town named Beachside Ave, "Lovefool" by The Cardigans plays. It triggers something in my brain, but I can't quite place what movie it's from. Kyle is softly singing along, and I laugh.

"What is this from?"

"*Romeo + Juliet*."

"Ah, yes. The one with Leo."

"I saw this movie at the drive-in theater…"

I shake my head. "Exactly how old are you again?"

"Hey, you know full well I'm only two years older than you. Smartass." His brow furrows dramatically. "If you would let me finish, I saw it as a kid. I must've been five or six at the time. My mom…" He laughs. "Well, first of all, she thought we were going to see *Space Jam*."

"A classic." I smile, settling back as I enjoy the warmth of the car and watching Kyle tell a story.

"You've seen it?"

"No, absolutely not."

"Ah, yes. Your sports aversion." His dimple pops.

"It's not an aversion. I don't get it. People chase a ball and everyone—not even just the people playing, but absolutely everyone—gets so upset."

"Usually one of the teams is happy."

I slice through the air. "You're getting off topic. You were going to see *Space Jam*."

"Right. So we drove pretty far up the coast to the drive-in that's near the border of Oregon and Washington. By the time we got there, I had fallen asleep, and my mom really had no interest in Bugs Bunny or Michael Jordan. So she bought tickets to *Romeo + Juliet.*"

"Seems fair." I see the street we need to turn down and point to take a left there.

He turns the car. "But I woke up as soon as the movie started. It was half an hour in before my mom realized I was awake. She was going to move the car to *Space Jam,* but I begged her to stay. So we watched it. It was amazing. The colors, the music, the guns. John Leguizamo's red vest. I was a changed man."

I laugh. "Oh no."

He nods. "Oh yes. I cut the sleeves off one of my red shirts and ran around the neighborhood with my water pistols, dropping to my knees and ripping off my makeshift vest, like he did in the gas station scene."

I can't stop laughing. A rogue tear streams down my face when I picture little Kyle in a homemade vest, pretending to be Tybalt. "What did the other kids think?"

"They loved it. We usually played cops and robbers, so they made me the robber."

I wipe away another tear and catch my breath. "I always pegged you for a cop."

"Hey…"

"No, not like that. You're just inherently good."

"Even good guys like to be a little bad sometimes," he says with a sly grin I haven't seen from him before.

It sends shivers down my spine.

I point to a large blue Victorian house lined with tasteful white Christmas lights.

Kyle pulls over to the curb. The little sign says *Martha's Bed and Breakfast* in a loopy script that is so ornate, it's almost impossible to read. My pulse quickens. Heather booked all the rooms for herself and me. We've been friends literally forever. We've shared a bed before. What if she booked a room with only one bed?

Kyle is unbuckling, completely unfazed. "Ready?"

We head up the porch steps, the third one from the top letting out a massive haunted house creak. That can't be a good sign.

Kyle opens the door, holding it for me as I walk into the entryway and am immediately hit with the delightful smell of gingerbread. A waist-high Nutcracker missing the tip of its nose holds a sign that says *Check-in* and has an arrow. I follow it to a room with a roaring fire in the fireplace, a sitting area, a piano, and shelves and shelves of books. In the corner is a large Christmas tree with antique ornaments. And toward the back of the room is a buffet table set up as a counter.

A woman is sitting with her feet propped up by the fire, reading. I step a little farther into the room, and Kyle comes in behind me, exclaiming, "Wow."

The woman drops her book, her slippered feet hitting the Persian rug. "Bless my stars, you startled me." She heads behind the counter. "You must be the young couple checking in."

"No," I say, the word flying out of my mouth.

Her face puckers. "Oh, well, I'm not sure I have any vacancies on account of the festival."

Kyle steps up, putting a hand on the small of my back. "We have a reservation, Mrs...."

Her smile is back, even brighter as she gazes at Kyle. "Ms. Renaurd."

"Ms. Renaurd. Lovely. Is that French?"

"My mother was French Canadian. Lived in Montreal most of her life."

We are getting off track. I nudge Kyle's foot. And he nudges me right back, nodding and listening patiently as Ms. Renaurd gives her entire Ancestry.com report.

"Fascinating," Kyle says with a genuine smile. "We have a reservation under McVeigh, but we aren't a couple."

"Ooh," Ms. Renaurd says, her eyebrows raising all the way up to her gray hair. She isn't seriously hitting on Kyle, is she?

"Yes. So we were hoping you might have a second room available."

Ms. Renaurd clicks and clacks on her keyboard, shaking her head.

"Sorry, hon. Like I said, the festival starts tomorrow. We do have a room with two beds. It's booked to a couple coming in, but I'm sure they wouldn't mind the upgrade. I usually only check it out to families with children. But it's so busy this time of year, I made an exception. It's a bit on the smaller side…"

I jump in. "That's perfect. We'll take it."

Kyle looks at me like maybe we should've discussed this, but I give him a megawatt smile.

We follow Ms. Renaurd up the grand center staircase, the dark-wood banister wrapped in fresh pine boughs and thick velvet ribbons, making everything smell absolutely heavenly. Once we get to the second floor, we walk down the hall, past all the doors, to another set of stairs—this one narrow, steep, and dark. There's no carpet runner to soften the thunk of our footsteps on the spiraled steps. There's one door at the top. Ms. Renaurd slips the old metal key inside.

It's dark until Ms. Renaurd crosses and clicks on the standing lamp. The room is like something out of an antique dollhouse and just as small. There's a fireplace that's about the largest thing in the whole place. On the far wall is a window overlooking the street below. Opposite the wall with the fireplace is a bunk bed. The top bunk looks like an awfully tight squeeze. It's quite close to the bottom of the dramatic slope of the dark exposed rafters.

There are a few floor pillows by the fireplace, and a large circular rug covers the dark hardwood floors.

Ms. Renaurd points to a blue door in the corner. "There's a washroom right through there with clean towels. Firewood is kept here." She opens a chest next to the fireplace.

I nod. This will be fine. Heather booked two nights, but if we can find Liam tonight, we only really need to stay one. I pull out my phone, scrolling to the Wi-Fi.

"What's the Wi-Fi password?" I ask as Kyle sets his bag down and frowns at the bunk bed. It does look quite small lengthwise.

Ms. Renaurd shakes her head. "None."

"No password?" No channel is coming up on my phone.

"No, dear. No Wi-Fi."

My phone has one tiny bar of service—5G isn't even up. I don't even think I could make a phone call in this dollhouse of a room, let alone try to access our—or rather, Heather's—master plan for this craziness.

I look at Kyle, not entirely sure what my face is doing, but he comes close to me and whispers in my ear, "Maybe she *knows* who we're looking for?"

Right. Small town. That's a great idea. "Ms. Renaurd, do you know a man named Liam Woodson?"

Her brow furrows. "No. Sorry. I took this place over from my mom a few years ago. Still getting to know people in town. And if they don't attend Beachside Christian Fellowship, I don't know them. I'll let you two get settled."

My heart sinks, and I let my body sink with it onto one of the floor cushions by the fireplace as Ms. Renaurd heads for the door. But Kyle steps in her way, ever so slightly. "Is there anywhere nearby that does have Wi-Fi?"

She smiles. "Of course. The Berry Beach Café down the street has it. They open first thing in the morning."

Kyle nods. "Anything that might be open tonight?"

"Well…" She runs a hand on the back of her neck. "Billy's Tavern about four blocks over toward the water might. I'm really not sure. I've never been there myself. They'll be open, though."

"Thank you so much."

Ms. Renaurd squeezes Kyle's arm and makes a little face. Like a *heavens-to-Betsy-my-my-my* face. I roll my eyes, shaking my head, which makes Kyle smirk. She heads out.

Kyle flexes dramatically as he points to the door. "The bar is thatta way."

I laugh, and he pulls me up off the floor.

"Come on. At the very least, we can get a drink and some food."

CHAPTER 7

The walk to Billy's is a quick and cold four blocks. Christmas lights wrap all the trees, lampposts, and about anything with form and shape along the street.

Billy's is a stone tavern with a heavy wooden door that wouldn't look out of place in an episode of *Game of Thrones*. Kyle holds the door open for me with a slight grimace.

"It really is as heavy as it looks."

I laugh. "Maybe you should start working out."

"Hey, I work out."

I cross my arms. "Moving kegs at the bar does not constitute weightlifting."

Kyle grabs the door with his other hand. "I do other stuff. I should've taken Ms. Renaurd. She appreciates my muscles. Come on. We're letting the cold in."

Walking into the bar is like walking into a toaster. Not just the heat, but Christmas lights cover every inch from floor to ceiling, giving the whole place a reddish glow against all the dark wood. We head straight to the bar and sit on two of the only empty seats in the place. The bartender asks what we'd like. I order a red wine, and Kyle orders an IPA.

The bartender gives me a heavy pour and a half smile. I nod my thanks but try not to make too much eye contact. He seems to be flirting with me, but maybe it's my imagination. Maybe that's my problem. I think everyone who's even semi-friendly is in love with me. Well, except for Kyle. I'm positive he doesn't see me that way.

Kyle's voice breaks into my thoughts, which were threatening to turn into a stroll down a dark memory alley. He asks the bartender, "Do you have Wi-Fi here?"

"Nah, man." The bartender points back and forth between us. "We're more 'bout talking to one another than scrolling."

I want to jump in and defend Kyle. He's about the furthest thing from a mindless scroller you can get. When you hang out with Kyle, he gives you his full attention. But the bartender has already walked away. Probably for the best. I don't need to alienate every person I meet along the way on this insane quest.

Turning to sit with my back against the bar, I sip my wine and let my muscles relax for a minute. Every table in the place and the dance floor are full. People are drinking, laughing, and checking out the old wooden stage with two lonely guitars on stands.

Kyle holds up his beer toward the stage. "Looks like we're in for some music."

I swallow a large sip of my wine. "Yikes."

Kyle smiles at me. "It could be good."

"You're such an optimist."

Kyle sits up straighter. "You know what? I am an optimist. And I don't see that there's anything wrong with that."

"Until it's clobbered," I say without even thinking. "Then what?"

He slouches back. His face is lit by the overhead Christmas lights, and his eyes are thoughtful. "Trust me, I've been let down many times. But I don't think anticipating the worst actually makes it any better if it happens. All it does is ruin the good time you could've been having."

His words slip right under my skin. It's surprising, really. Mostly, words tend to slide off me, but his sink in like butter on bread straight from the oven. What has expecting the worst really done for me? All my worrying didn't stop Grandma from getting sick, not the first, not the second, and certainly not the third time.

"You could be right," I say softly.

He leans in dramatically. "What was that?"

I sigh. "Don't let it go to your head."

"Too late. You have to be a little bit optimistic, right? To go on this trip. You must be hoping that seeing one of these old flames might spark something again. Give it a second chance." Kyle looks at me with his deep-brown eyes.

I sputter on my wine. "What? No, that's not what this is about at all." I shake my head for emphasis. "No sparks, no flame, no burning at all."

Kyle turns in his seat to face me more head-on. "What is it about, then?"

That's a great question. And after rearranging his plans and driving all this way knowing so little of the actual plan, he deserves a real answer. I sigh. "Heather said I left them all heartbroken."

He nods. "I remember you asking about that."

"I guess…" I want to prove to myself that that's not true. But that sounds so dumb and selfish. It's not all about my feelings. I want to make sure they're okay, too. To make sure I wasn't so careless that I left lasting damage. "I didn't want to ambush them with a phone call so close to the holidays."

It's partly true.

"Ahhh, more about the good ol' in-person ambush."

"No, it's not supposed to feel like an ambush at all. I'm going to pretend that running into them is a coincidence."

Kyle frowns, and my once-relaxed muscles are all wound up tight as pins again.

"Can we drop it for now?"

I fish out my phone. Maybe being in civilization—sort of—I'll have enough bars to pull up my email. Or the internet. But nope. No luck.

"Any service?" Kyle asks, looking at his own phone.

"Not a bar. You?"

He tucks his phone back into his jean jacket. "Nothing."

Shit. This whole adventure is starting to look like a really bad idea. Why didn't I look over the plan? Better yet, why didn't I write it down?

I take a hearty sip of my wine as the lights dim and people stand at their tables, cheering. Some have even moved to the space in front of the stage. Something in me snaps. Fuck it.

Downing the rest of my wine in one slightly painful go, I hold out my hand to Kyle. "Shall we?"

He smiles, setting his beer on the counter and placing a coaster over it. Kyle, apparently, is too smart to chug an IPA. He takes my hand, his palm warm and solid. "We shall."

We find a place to stand as three guys walk across the stage. Two pick up the guitars, and one sits behind the drums. As more people move to the space in front of the stage, the hardwood floors quiver under their footsteps. The first note plays, and the vibration rumbles through the crowd. I don't recognize the song, but it has a heavy base beat.

Kyle's smile is ear to ear, and I wonder if he feels it, too, this thrum of possibility. Like anything can happen.

He catches me watching him and does something I didn't even think possible—his smile grows even wider. He throws me a wink. My stomach does an odd and somewhat alarming dip. I thought I'd gotten over my crush on Kyle years ago.

I did. I have. It's just the odd situation we find ourselves in. What girl doesn't get a little zing at a wink, even from a friend?

Most of the crowd is on the dance floor by the second song, swaying and stomping. A large gentleman jostles by us, knocking slightly into my shoulder, and Kyle places a hand right above my waistband. I feel the heat of his palm radiate through my entire body.

A new song starts, and the throng moves into some kind of formation.

"Um, what is happening?" I ask as another person moves past us to join one of the lines.

Kyle takes my hand and leads me to one of the lines. "I think we're going to line dance, Ruby."

Backing up, I hold my hands up like I'm warding off a ferocious animal. "Uh-uh. I don't know how."

Kyle grabs me by the belt loops and pulls me back into the line with surprising force. "I don't know how to do it either. Come on." He releases my jeans and smiles. "We'll learn together."

Something settles in my chest. I can do this. Kyle and I have learned tons of things together. He showed me the ropes at the bar. Taught me how to make my first old fashioned. He taught me how to do my taxes. He helped me with the paperwork on the house once Grandma was gone.

We can do this.

I hook my thumbs through my belt loops and smile. "Okay."

We shuffle somewhat in unison, following along with the crowd. Kyle is getting the hang of it more so than I am. He moves with ease, almost like he's done this before, but he said he hasn't, and Kyle is honest to a fault. But boy, he sure can move.

Right foot, right foot, left foot, left foot. Right, left, and now everyone is turning. There's a lasso move, which is my personal favorite. Every time it comes up, my hips get in on the action. The third time I do it, Kyle whoops, and my stomach tightens. My blood is pumping, my heart racing, and my cheeks are flushed.

By the time the song is over, the back of my hair is damp with sweat. I pull it up into a messy bun. When I turn, Kyle's eyes are on me, and there's a heat to them that makes me want to pull him close, tug his face to mine.

He looks away quickly. "Another drink?"

I push the butterflies away. "Yes. Something cold."

We head back to the bar. Kyle's IPA is untouched through the magic of the balanced coaster. I order a Pabst from the bartender and take a much-needed seat on the stool.

"Whew." I wipe the sweat off my brow.

"You can say that again."

"Where'd you learn to move like that?"

Kyle's mid-drink. He takes a moment to swallow as a small bead of sweat runs down his neck. He sets his beer down. "Seventh grade gym class. We didn't line dance, though. It was ballroom."

My eyes widen as I picture gangly Kyle ballroom dancing. "No."

He laughs and rubs the back of his neck. "Yes."

I'm back on my feet, my heat and exhaustion completely forgotten. "Show me."

"Now?"

I grab his hand, tugging a little. The band is still playing, but it's a slow dance. Some people are standing near the stage, while others are swaying—cheek to cheek. "There's room in the back. Come on."

We go out onto the dance floor, and Kyle positions us. He places my hand on his shoulder, and the other is snug in his palm. His hand finds the small of my back. "Follow my lead. When I step forward, you step back."

I've always wanted to learn ballroom dance. *Dancing With the Stars* was a favorite of mine and Grandma's. I nod, looking at our feet. "Got it."

Kyle lets go of the hand holding mine and softly tilts my chin up. "Look up here. Connect to me. And the music. Your feet will do the right thing."

I look at him and follow his lead, stepping back when he steps forward. Turning when he turns. Kyle has such an interesting face. I think he's so handsome because it's not perfect. It has perfect elements. Strong square jaw, currently covered in a fine layer of dark stubble. High cheekbones. Really great hair. His hair looks like Superman's. Even customers call him Superman with brown eyes. But his nose, while completely lovely, is definitely what makes his face interesting. I once heard a regular say it looks like it's never backed down from a fight.

"Kyle?"

"Mmm."

"Have you ever been in a fight?"

He looks into my eyes instead of scanning our surroundings. Realization dawns, smoothing out the wrinkle between his brows. "Are you asking if I've broken my nose?"

Heat floods my cheeks. "Maybe."

"I have, and I did."

"What happened?" I ask as we turn to the music.

"It was the summer between sixth and seventh grade. I decided to compete in the sandcastle festival. My mom… She had died a couple months earlier, and she competed every year. I decided I was going to honor her by doing it in her place. I took it so seriously. I had sketches all over my wall with measurements and diagrams. It looked like I was trying to solve a murder."

"Detective Kyle and the case of the sandcastle."

He chuckles. "Exactly. Well, when it came time to compete, it didn't all go exactly as planned. I was making a pod of dolphins. Dolphins were my mom's favorite animal. There was one large dolphin in the middle and two smaller dolphins on each side. Despite practicing for weeks, I wasn't as skilled as I hoped to be. Some older boys came by and said it looked like a penis."

I'm so startled, I laugh. "What?"

"I've looked at the photos my dad took, and honestly, they weren't wrong. At the time, though, I saw red. I went straight up to the largest of the three and punched him square in the face."

I can't picture it. I've seen Kyle escort people out of the bar, but I can't picture him being violent. "Oh no."

He nods. "He punched me back, and it felt great."

"Breaking your nose felt great?"

"Nah, he didn't break my nose. He gave me a black eye. And it felt like a release. For once, I had a physical reason to be in so much pain, instead of this empty void."

I know that void well. I look into Kyle's eyes, and he goes on.

"After that, I picked fights with everyone. Kids at school. The guys playing for the other teams at baseball. Friends, even. I fought my way through middle school until I wound up in a jail cell. Picked a fight with the sheriff's son."

"Why?"

"Because he was always making fun of my buddy for being a little heavier. One day, outside Stonehouse, he called him fatty, and I punched him in the stomach. Now, *he* broke my nose. But not before I got some good shots in. Cops showed up at my door that night."

The song is over, and another one starts. Kyle drops my hand and takes a step back. "You can waltz."

"Thank you for showing me."

We head back to our beers.

"What made you stop fighting?"

Kyle fiddles with his glass on the bar. "My dad's face when the cop car drove away. He lost the love of his life, and here I was, making things harder. I didn't see it before, but I saw it clear as the stars that night. I couldn't do that to him. He'd been nothing but good. Trying to step in. Making sure we had meals on the table, even if more times than not, they were Hungry Man microwave dinners."

I smile. "What did you do instead? For the pain?"

The bartender comes over and grabs Kyle's empty glass and mine. "Need another round?"

Kyle looks at me.

I shake my head. "We should probably get going if we're going to track down Liam first thing."

"Liam Woodson?" the bartender asks.

"Yeah. You know him?" I say, my heart rate picking up.

"He's usually here for line dancing night. If he's not here, I'd check the hospital."

CHAPTER 8

"The hospital?" Picturing Liam tucked into a hospital bed, hooked up to machines, makes my palms sweat.

The bartender nods, handing Kyle the check. "He probably got called in."

Called in. I take the tab from Kyle, but he's already handed over his card. It clicks. "Liam is a doctor?"

The bartender hands another slip of paper and Kyle's card back to him. "A damn fine one from what my sister says."

"How far away is the hospital from here?" Kyle asks.

"A little less than a mile into the center of town."

Kyle raises his eyebrows at me.

I shrug. This is what we're here for after all, isn't it? The ring digs into my hip through my jeans pocket, almost as an answer. "Let's go."

Bundled up in our coats, we head down the road.

Pulling up the Lyft app on my phone, it won't load. I stare at the completely empty streets. There is not a soul around.

Kyle peers over my shoulder. "It's a nice night for a walk."

I put my phone away, shoving my hands farther into my pockets as I do. Trying to keep my teeth from chattering, I say, "Delightful."

The streets, though desolate, are beautiful. The Christmas lights twinkle. We're surrounded by the familiar scent of the sea.

It's too cold to talk. Despite the chill, my palms are sweating. What was I thinking, coming out here and tracking down Liam after all this time?

Kyle asks, "You okay?"

I inhale a deep breath of cold air. "I'm not sure."

"Fair." Kyle nods. "So, what's this guy's name again?"

"Liam."

"What's his deal?"

We pass the town square, where a bronze statue of a horse is wearing a Santa hat.

"Apparently, he's a doctor."

"No, I mean why are we tracking him down? What's the deal between the two of you?"

I shove my hands deeper in my pockets. "You're going to laugh."

"I won't. Cross my heart."

I look at his honest face and sigh. "We were boyfriend and girlfriend in the summer before tenth grade."

"Why would I laugh at that? Must've been pretty serious if you think he might've given you a ring."

"It was for a week."

"A week?" Kyle practically yells, his voice echoing in the clear night.

"It was summer camp. We were both junior counselors. Met the first day of training. He passed me a note at lunch. By dinner, we were an item."

"Wow. You move fast."

I brush off my shoulder. "What can I say? I was a very confident teenager."

Kyle's eyebrows rise. "Really?"

"No. He liked me, and I ran with it. I made him friendship bracelets with my campers in arts and crafts. He made me a box in wood shop. We were the *it couple* of the summer."

"So, then what happened?"

Spotting a building straight out of a black-and-white movie, I look closer. It's brick with white marble Art Deco details and two white marble lions in front of modern-looking automatic doors. There's a sign out front that reads *Hospital*. Pointing, I say, "There it is."

I run—to escape the cold and Kyle's question. Two birds, one stone.

Kyle follows me. I slow down right as I reach the automatic doors.

The overhead fluorescent lights are too bright, especially after coming in from the dark. The air doesn't just smell of disinfectant—it's laced with it. Like my lungs are getting cleaned by breathing it in. Cleaned or damaged.

As I walk farther in toward the reception desk, my throat feels tight. I haven't stepped foot in a hospital since Grandma died. Not even when I sliced my thumb pretty good doing prep at the bar. It probably needed stitches, but I couldn't walk through the door. The woman at the desk is focused on the screen in front of her. I'm nearly to the check-in counter when a door opens and shuts. The little sound of compressed air triggers something in my brain. I swivel on my heel, turn around, and head past Kyle right out the door.

The cold air is fresh and filled with smells beyond rubbing alcohol. I gulp it in and march back across the street, taking a seat on a bench in the square. The metal is so cold, it zings my thighs.

Kyle runs out of the hospital, looking frantic until he spots me. He walks over and takes a seat. But he doesn't say anything. He just sits, leans back, and drapes his arm across the back of the bench, gazing up at the sky.

After a few minutes, my heart rate slows. I shove my hair behind my ear and say, "Hospitals."

Kyle nods. "I get it. My mom hated them, too. Every time we had to go to Fortune Falls General for chemo, she tried to cancel. Literally. She'd tell me she couldn't go because there was too much to do at home. The bathrooms had to be cleaned, or the sheets needed to be washed. I'd tell her if she didn't go, I'd swallow window cleaner. Then we'd have to go to the hospital anyway."

I laugh. "You didn't."

He chuckles, rubbing a hand over his mouth. "I did. I thought I knew everything. In the end, it didn't matter anyway. I should've let her stay home."

My heart breaks in my chest. I put a hand on Kyle's knee. "You couldn't have known that."

He nods, biting his lip. "Yeah, well…I just meant to say I understand the whole hospital thing."

I move my hand from his leg, placing both in my lap. "Why does it have to smell like that?"

"Right? Has no one invented lavender disinfectant?"

I nod. "Or maybe a nice gingerbread for the holidays."

"Exactly."

We fall into silence, and I look up at the stars.

"My grandma didn't seem to mind going. I'm sure she hated it, but she never said. She'd bake cookies to share. It's just…" Tears prick the back of my eyes, and I shake my head, trying to force them back. "It's just hard."

Kyle grabs my hand—his is surprisingly warm. He gives mine a little squeeze. "We don't have to go in there. We can wait for his day off. Shit, we can stay right here and stake out the place until his shift is over."

I laugh. "We'll freeze to death."

Kyle moves a little closer to me on the bench, wrapping his arm around me. I can feel the heat of his thigh through my jeans as his leg presses into mine. "We'll be okay."

We sit like that for a couple of minutes. Suddenly, with the warmth from Kyle's body, I'm so tired. I lay my head on his shoulder.

"Or we could go back to the room," he says, his voice hoarse.

It's like an electric zap. I move my head off his shoulder and stand from the bench.

"To sleep." He holds up both hands. "It's been a long day."

My eyes are fixed on the hospital doors. "No. I can do this. Let's go."

This time, I don't stop to take in the sights and smells of the hospital. Instead, I march right up to the reception desk and put my hands on the counter. "I'm here to see Liam Woodson."

The woman behind the desk looks at me from behind her purple-rimmed glasses like I'm nuts. Honestly, I'm not sure she's wrong.

"Doctor Woodson," I clarify—unnecessarily, I realize, because the woman's expression doesn't change.

"He's a bit busy at the moment." The woman turns her attention back to the screen.

"It's an emergency." What am I even saying? Whatever this is, emergency it is not.

The woman points to the left. "ER is right over there, sweetie."

"No." I sigh. "Not that kind." I dig the ring out of my pocket, fiddling with it between my thumb and forefinger.

She stares at me, and my face is reflected back in the lenses of her glasses. My blonde hair wild around my face, my eyes desperate. I don't know if it's the drinks, the adrenaline letdown from the dancing, or the stars outside shining down on this clear night. Something snaps. Everything comes tumbling out—and I mean everything. Not only about the love-life list, or the hunting down my exes map, but about Grandma, too. About how empty the house has been since she passed and how finding the ring felt like a sign from her.

"Oh, sweetie," the woman says, grabbing a tissue and dabbing her eyes. "I get it. I lost my mother this last spring."

"I'm so sorry."

We share a moment of silence that neither of us immediately tries to fill.

"A long time ago, Liam—sorry, Dr. Woodson—and I…" I trail off, not sure how to explain. "I'm not trying to stir up trouble. I just want to talk to him. Ask him a few questions. Get some closure."

She bites her lip, looking at the ceiling. "Look, I really shouldn't do this, but he's on floor three. There's a waiting room up there. You should run into him."

"Oh my goodness, thank you. Thank you. Thank you."

She sits up straighter. "Don't make me regret this."

I give her a firm nod. "Nope. No regrets."

Kyle is hanging around by a bulletin board. He comes over to me once I catch his eye, and we make our way to the elevators.

"He's on the third floor. She said if we wait there, we'll run into him."

Kyle smiles. "Perfect."

The elevator comes quickly, and despite the age of the building, it's a smooth, quiet ride to the third floor. The waiting room is darker than downstairs. Lit by lamps instead of fluorescents. There's an older couple sitting in the corner. The man has his eyes glued to the television in the corner showing an old episode of *MythBusters*. The woman is knitting a small yellow bootie.

In the distance, there is the faint cry of a baby. I take a seat in the opposite corner from the older couple. The beige chair is surprisingly comfortable. Or maybe I'm just so tired that any seat with a cushion suddenly feels like a five-star hotel mattress.

Kyle crooks his thumb. "I'm going to try to find a vending machine. Want anything?"

I shrug off my coat, laying it across my lap. "My pajamas."

"Ha. You and me both. We can leave if you want…"

I shake my head. "Nah, I was kidding. Well, I wasn't, but… We should stay. If that's okay?" I look into Kyle's tired face.

He smiles. "Totally okay. I'm here if you're here. I need a Snickers."

He heads off to locate some sugar. Idly, I slip the ring onto my finger, twisting it around. Maybe this whole thing is crazy.

I pull out my phone, and a brilliant idea occurs to me: Wi-Fi. Hospitals have Wi-Fi. I open my settings. After a few clicks and identifying all the bicycles in a photograph, I'm on.

When I scroll to my email, it miraculously opens, and there it is. Heather's master plan. And of course, I have no paper nor pen on me. But it doesn't matter. I take screenshots, making sure I get all of it and start to read.

Liam Woodson is a doctor!

Yes, we've established that.

He is married with three kids and one on the way.

Holy shit. I can't even imagine having one child right now, let alone three. But at the ripe old age of thirty-two, I guess it's something I need to start thinking about soon-ish. A small part of me has always wanted a family. Little hands helping me knead the dough. Laughter at Christmas.

I'm about to read the next line and save my existential crisis for later when a man in green scrubs walks down the hallway and heads straight for the older couple.

He takes off his mask, his smile wide and oh-so-familiar. It's Liam. More lines around his smile, a few grays in his hair, and Lord have mercy, more muscles in his forearms, but it is undoubtedly him.

"It's a boy," he says in a deeper voice than I remember.

The woman jumps up, clapping, while the older man nods.

"We can go back and see them now." He motions to the hallway, and the couple gets up, the woman practically running.

I stand, moving forward. This is it. This is my shot. "Liam."

CHAPTER 9

He turns, and his eyes land on me. At first, his face doesn't change as he looks me up and down in an almost clinical way. When they land on my face again, his eyes widen a smidge. Enough that I know he recognizes me.

Liam holds up a finger to me and turns to the older couple. "Do you remember the way?"

The older man chuckles. "She's already halfway there, Doc."

The couple moves down the hall, while Liam's gaze returns to me. His blue eyes are filled with…disbelief, maybe?

"Ruby McVeigh."

"Liam Woodson."

"This is a surprise. Do you know Melanie?" He points down the hallway.

"Actually, I came to see you." God, so much for lying and saying this was all some big coincidence running into each other. But what other reason would I have to be in the maternity ward at eleven o'clock at night?

Liam motions to the chairs, and we both take a seat. He scrubs a hand over his face, and I can hear the sound of the stubble prickling his soft palm. I wonder how long he's been here tonight.

"I can't believe it's you. Your hair is as wild as ever." He tugs a stray curl then pulls his hand back like it's electrified. "I'm married. Happily. I mean, not that that's why you're here." He lets out a heavy sigh, and I jump in.

"It's not like that. I'm not here to rekindle anything. I wondered…"

At the end of summer camp, we exchanged addresses and a passionate—or what I thought at the time to be—kiss. We were both sixteen, and all we did was kiss, but man were we good at it. I headed to the parking lot to my car, and he walked to the buses. But I couldn't help myself. I just needed one more kiss. I ran back and saw him with a petite girl with short black hair. They were holding each other so close and kissing, which was so clearly *our* thing.

I ran as fast as I could, not looking back this time. Liam wrote just like he said he would. For months, envelopes would arrive—sometimes large manilla ones bulging with unseen goodies, sometimes dainty pink ones. I never opened a single one. They're all in that stupid breakup case. It stands to reason this ring on my finger could've fallen out of one of them.

I hold up my hand, the diamond catching the light of the lamp. "Is this from you?"

Liam takes my hand. His are cold and dry. He looks so closely at the ring that my heart stops. This is it. It was this easy. Liam sent me the ring in one of those many letters. I can give it back. He'll say he's sorry he was a two-timing dick all those years ago, and we can all feel better. Kyle and I can head back home…to our respective homes. Everything will go back to normal.

My limbs suddenly feel as heavy as a full keg at the bar.

Liam drops my hand. "No. I did send a ring, but it was a little fifteen-dollar silver thing I got from a flea market. It had a little red stone on it."

We both say, "Ruby."

Liam swallows hard. "Did you ever get my letters?"

I nod.

"Why didn't you ever write back?"

Sitting up straighter, I look him square in his light-blue eyes. We always thought it was so cool we had nearly the same shade and said if we ever had kids, they would also have the same. I push the thought away. "I saw you."

His gaze remains steady, completely unaffected by this revelation.

I throw my hands down. "I saw you kissing that girl with the Winona Ryder haircut."

Liam laughs. He actually laughs. "We weren't kissing. It was a hug."

A hug? I search my memory. Sunlight skimming through the branches, the smell of campfires being put out, people laughing. Liam and this girl, their faces so close, they absolutely had to be kissing.

"You were making out." There's a tight ball in my chest. How can he not remember what happened?

"No, we weren't."

I stand. I don't have to sit here and listen to these lies. "Look, it was a long time ago. Maybe you just can't remember."

Liam stands, too. God, he's a lot taller than I remember. "I'm one hundred percent certain I did not kiss that girl."

"How can you possibly remember? It was nearly fifteen years ago." And I know what I saw, I think but don't say.

"She's my sister." Liam frowns.

"Your sister?"

He nods, crossing his arms. "She was a camper, and she was really sad camp was over. I gave her a big hug, and she snotted all over my shirt. It was the shirt that you said made my eyes look like the shallow part of the ocean. I was so pissed she ruined it."

"Why didn't you tell me you had a sister?"

"Pretty sure I did. She was in the Shooting Stars cabin."

Shit. The tightness in my chest sinks to the pit of my stomach. That sounds familiar. Shit.

"You did." I collapse back into one of the nearby chairs.

Liam sits, too, but he's perched on the edge of the seat, like he's getting ready to go.

"Why didn't you ask me about it?"

I was so sure that Liam had found someone better. So sure that what we had wasn't real. It was more fuel to my fire that relationships aren't worth the trouble. But I'd gotten it all wrong.

"I thought I knew exactly what was going on." I shake my head. "I'm sorry."

He smiles. "It's okay. We were teenagers."

We were. But how many other times have I been so certain of something that isn't at all true?

Liam gives my hair another small tug. "I have to check on my patient. Are you sticking around?"

I stand and brush my hands off on my jeans. "No."

He nods and purses his lips to the side. "It was nice to see you again." He sighs. "Honestly, it's nice to know what happened. Thank you for that."

I smile, and he returns it before he walks down the hall, disappearing around the corner.

I FIND Kyle by the vending machine, leaning against the wall, munching a Snickers bar and looking at his phone. He hands me a bag of Peanut M&M's, my favorite.

"Was he the guy? I saw you two talking. I didn't want to interrupt."

"No, it wasn't him." There's a soul-crushing heaviness in my limbs, and without warning, tears start to roll down my cheeks. What the fuck is happening?

Kyle rushes over and puts an arm around my shoulders. "Hey, it's okay. We'll find who it's from."

I swipe the tears away, but more return in their place. "I don't know why I'm so upset."

Kyle pulls me in closer, and I inhale deeply as I lay my head on his shoulder. That spicy woodsmoke and wool smell surrounds me.

We stand there like that for a few moments. His jean jacket is rough on my cheek, his hands warm on my back.

"Were you hoping it was him?"

"No."

"Were you hoping this would all be over if it was?"

I shake my head and look up. Kyle is gazing into my face. His eyes are so warm, so familiar, so...

I pull back abruptly and smile to soften the cold rush of air between us. "I think I'm just tired."

"Let's head back to the B&B."

THE WALK BACK IS LONG, cold, and quiet. The actual time in minutes is probably only twenty, but in the amount of silence and frigid air, it takes eons. We climb the narrow stairs to our tiny room. It's almost as cold as it was outside.

Kyle motions to the hearth. "I'll start a fire."

I shrug off my coat and immediately regret it. Grabbing my pajamas from my bag, I ask, "Mind if I shower?"

Kyle waves his hand, but his focus stays on his task.

The bathroom is cute. Sage-green tile covers the floor, a knotted red rug thrown over it. There's a circular window, and the walls are covered in different-sized mirrors, some with gold frames, some with plastic pink ones. It's eclectic but fun. There's a sink, a toilet, and a clawfoot tub with absolutely no showerhead.

My bones are tired. I really want to hop into a quick shower and get into my pajamas. But it looks like the only option is to take a bath.

Placing my pajamas on the sink, I start to take off my shirt. I'll just get into fresh clothes and crawl into bed. But as soon as the cold air hits my skin, I change my mind. Fine. I turn both knobs at the same time, the hot a little more than the cold. Okay, a lot more. I sit on the edge of the tub and watch the bath fill with water as the room fills with heavenly steam.

How could I have been so wrong about what happened with Liam? I was positive he'd kissed her, positive he'd misled me.

When I got home from camp, Grandma was almost back to her old self after another round of chemo. Her hair had grown back, short and curlier than before. She was puttering around the garden again, but slower than before. Not a lot, just enough that I noticed. So when I got letter after letter from who I thought was a liar and a cheater, in the grand scheme of things, it didn't seem that important.

I went to my grandma's every day for the rest of the summer until school was back in session. We baked, and she tried for the billionth time to teach me to garden. I should've asked Liam what happened, I really should've, but my time wasn't wasted.

As I sink into the hot water, my whole body eases. I wasn't aware of how tense and flexed everything was until it relaxes. I let my mind drift. Liam is an actual grown-up now. He has a family of his own. He has a grown-up job, helping bring life into the world. And what do I do? Hand people beers. Make the odd martini. Bake at my home alone. I bake so much, I don't even have enough friends to share it with. But what else would I do with my life?

We all live, we work, we die. What does it really matter what the work is?

This closure doesn't feel as good as the one with Josh. Instead, it seems a lot of things I was certain of aren't as they seemed.

CHAPTER 10

After my fingers are properly pruned, I drain the tub and step out. I slip into my red buffalo print flannel pajamas and then brush my teeth. Through the door, I hear an odd *click, click, click.* I turn off the water and listen more closely. *Click, click, click.*

A cloud of steam follows me as I leave the bathroom. Kyle is sitting cross-legged on one of the floor pillows by the fire in light-gray sweats and a snug black thermal. His hands are moving back and forth at a swift pace—knitting.

The man is knitting. The dark-red yarn moving between his fingers looks deliciously soft. I take a seat on the opposite floor cushion and tug on my fuzzy socks with puffball snowmen at the top.

"Feel better?" Kyle asks without looking up from his needles.

"How long have you been doing this?" I'm still shocked. I've known Kyle for years, and I didn't know he knits.

"Just since you got in the bath."

"No, I mean in your life. How did I not know you knit?"

He shrugs. "It's something I do before bed. It calms me."

"Ahhh," I say, half lying down in front of the fire. The flames are brushing Kyle's cheeks with a golden glow. "Is this what you do instead of beating people up?"

Kyle smirks. "It's part of it."

"What's the other part?"

His smirk grows wider. "Wouldn't you like to know?"

I settle farther on my side, staring into the flames, the rhythmic click clacking of Kyle's needles a soothing metronome. "What do you make?"

"Mostly, I make scarves, but I've made a mitten or two. It's nice to have something to do with my hands. Plus, the yarn is soft."

He holds out the end of the scarf. My fingers brush against his as I reach out to feel. It's happened a billion times before at the bar, handing off a glass or a bottle, even at my place while sharing popcorn, but the way his eyes flick to mine and the way I can't look away feels very different. The yarn is velvety between my fingers. The noise comes out of me as a pure reaction. From the texture of the yarn or the heat of Kyle's gaze, I'm not sure. "Mmmm."

Kyle's pupils double in size. His lips—how have I never noticed how plump and sexy his lips are?—are parted slightly. We both freeze, the air as thick as when I was in the bath.

If this were anyone else, I'd toss his yarn aside and kiss him. But this is Kyle. My coworker. My friend. My *best* friend besides Heather. We can't. I can't. Things'll get weird, and I need him. As a friend.

I sit up straight and yawn, even though after that heady moment, I'm not the least bit tired. "Oof. I'm pooped. I'm going to turn in."

I stand and come face to face with the bunk bed. It doesn't even look long enough for Kyle to fit on without curling into a little ball. But that's not my problem. I'm going to lie down, close my eyes, and go to sleep. I'm not sure which one Kyle would prefer, though. Since he's already going to be uncomfortable, I'll let him pick. "Top or bottom?"

"I usually let the lady lead on that front."

My cheeks warm. "Such a gentleman."

I dive onto the bottom bunk and lie awake with my eyes closed tight, willing sleep to take me.

THE SOUND of feet shuffling on the hardwood floor wakes me up. It's unusual, not like walking or pacing. I turn toward the middle of the room, opening my eyes and immediately closing them. I must've slept late. Golden sunlight coming in from the window fills the room, visible even through my eyelids because it's so bright.

I open my eyes again, this time a little slower. Kyle is in front of the fire, his long arms outstretched, his front leg bent, his back leg stretched out long.

Shirtless.

His core is flexed. He has a lot of abs. Holy shit. How have I never noticed this while swimming at the lake in the summer? He has like… an eight-pack. He raises his arms up toward the ceiling and brings his back leg to meet his front, squatting down as if sitting in an invisible chair. His gray sweats are slung low on his hips.

Sitting up, I forget the whole tiny bunk bed thing and smack my head on the bed frame. Immediately, I lie back down, hand on my forehead.

Kyle rushes over, kneeling by the bed. "You okay?"

"Yeah. Don't mind me. Concussing myself is my favorite thing to do first thing in the morning."

Kyle reaches for my hand on my forehead, moving it away gently. He's looking so intently at the spot. If it weren't so sweet, it'd be funny. "It's a little red, but no goose egg. Want me to track down some ice?"

"I'll be okay."

He backs up, and I get out of bed, scooting off to the bathroom. After I wash my face, I inspect the spot. There's a small red circle, but I'll live.

When I head back into the room, Kyle has both toes pointed out. He's squatting like he's riding a horse. His hands are up by his chest, pressed together like he's praying, and his eyes are closed.

I stand right next to him.

Without opening his eyes, he moves to stand, placing one foot on his upper thigh. "Did I wake you?"

"Maybe." I try to do the same movement but can't keep my

balance. I catch myself, placing both feet on the floor. Taking a steadying breath, I try again. Using my hand, I put my left foot on my right thigh and keep my hands out for extra balance.

"In my defense," Kyle says with his eyes still closed, "it *is* nearly ten a.m."

I shrug, not that he can see it. "Bar hours. I sleep late. Why don't you sleep late?" I mimic his stance as best I can, bringing my hands together.

He opens his eyes and smiles. "Do you do much yoga?"

"No."

"Really? You're a natural." His smile grows so wide, it takes up the whole room.

"You're so full of shit." My legs wobble as if to prove my point, and my foot hits the floor. "Come on, what am I doing wrong?"

Kyle moves to stand behind me, placing his hands on my waist. "Bring your foot up. It doesn't have to be so high, though. It could be to your ankle or calf."

I place my foot on my knee, and Kyle's hands move down, skimming my hips. He moves my foot to just above my ankle. His touch is soft but firm. "Right here is perfect."

He moves back to standing, and my body feels the absence of his hands like a loss. My skin is cold where his hands were. Like leaving a warm blanket behind in the morning.

"You got it."

I'd been so focused on everything else, I didn't even realize I was doing it. I'm balanced. And I immediately fall out of it.

Kyle grabs my elbow, catching me from tumbling to the ground. I stumble into him, my hands on his bare chest. As soon as his skin touches mine, it's like being back under the warmth of the comforter. Kyle is solid. I knew he was strong, but I had no idea he had this many muscles. I tilt my face up toward him, and his warm brown eyes are staring right back at me.

I move away, shocked by how much I want him to keep touching me. It's abrupt, the movement.

Kyle's smile falls. He moves across the room, grabbing his shirt and tugging it on. "I'm going to shower."

"No shower. Only a bath."

Kyle sighs. "Ah, great."

He heads into the bathroom. Once the door clicks shut, I lie back down on the bed with a heavy sigh. What is wrong with me? Why am I suddenly lusting after my good friend like we're back in high school?

It's the holidays. And the cramped room. And all this delving into my love life. My ghosts of relationships past. That's all it is.

After dressing in jeans and a thick red sweater, I have a seat on one of the floor cushions. Pulling up my screenshots, I copy down the plan into my notebook. I will not be foiled by technology again. We only have one more ex to see. We can figure out if this ring is from him or not and then head back to Fortune Falls.

Kyle comes out of the bathroom dressed in dark jeans and a forest-green plaid shirt that hugs his broad shoulders. "So, what's the plan, Captain?"

"Right." I read back over my notes. "Well, Heather didn't think we'd be able to track Liam down so quickly. She booked us for two nights here. But we could probably check out early and maybe get a refund?" I sigh.

"Where's the next stop?" Kyle asks, sitting on the floor and lacing up his boots.

"Leavenworth."

Kyle nods. "Might be hard to get a room there this time of year."

Leavenworth is basically Christmastown for the Pacific Northwest. "She got us one, somehow. But it's not booked until tomorrow night."

Kyle stands and looks out the window.

I put my notebook in my bag, shooing away my Libra indecisive-ness. "This is what we should do. We should see if we can check out today. Head up to Leavenworth and find Nick. Maybe we won't even have to stay the night. And if we do, I'm sure this place Heather booked will have room for us early. It's the Friday before Christmas. People have to go to their jobs. Who's holiday adventuring besides two temporarily out of work bartenders on a *Lord of the Rings*–style quest?"

"I don't know where this newfound optimism is coming from, and I hate to discourage it." Kyle chuckles as he turns away from the window. "But the Friday before Christmas is prime holiday adventure time. While it's sound logic that people would be at their jobs on a Friday, I'm not sure that's the case. It might be tricky getting out of here today."

"What makes you say that?"

He points out the window.

I head over to look. Wooden stands line the streets, draped in Christmas lights and pine boughs. They stretch as far down as I can see. People are strolling down the middle of the road holding steaming paper cups. A child, gripping his mother's coat with one hand and clutching a stuffed Rudolph in the other, skips, his cheeks rosy, eyes wide.

"It'll be fine," I say. "There has to be a way out of town. We'll get some coffee, check out, and hit the road."

Kyle nods. "Aye, aye, Captain."

As we head down the stairs, I nearly fall to my knees with the overwhelming smell of bacon. "We might need food not from a vending machine, too."

"Agreed," Kyle says in a husky voice that sends a shiver down my spine. The man must really love bacon.

I approach the desk and ring the little bell, the ring hardly audible over Mariah Carey crooning about what she wants for Christmas.

Kyle points. "Dining room."

We walk through the entryway and across the hall to a homey room, just as cute as the lobby. In the corner, there's a flocked tree with shiny light-blue bobbles. White tablecloths, detailed with blue snowflake borders, adorn the round tables. Out the large bay window, there's an even better view of the street fair. For such a small town, it's packed.

Ms. Renaurd is filling up guests' cups from a silver coffee pot, wearing a bright-red apron like a regular Mrs. Claus. She gives me a slight head nod. Her eyes find Kyle, and she smiles, raising her hand even while pouring with the other. She heads over to us, her hips swinging in a way they weren't a second ago. She even adjusts her white V-neck sweater so it's a smidge lower.

I mean, Kyle is hot. He is. It's the hair—he has luscious, thick black hair—and his deep-brown eyes look like melted chocolate. His jawline is so sharp it could cut you if you got too close. I acknowledge that it is an undeniable fact that he is hot. *But come on.* This is a little much.

"How did you sleep?" she asks, eyes solely focused on Kyle.

"Great." He smiles, and it doesn't help matters.

Ms. Renaurd practically swoons.

"Liar," I say under my breath. There's no way he slept well on that mattress he hardly fit on. Plus, he was knitting when I fell asleep and yogaing when I woke up. I'm not even sure he went to sleep.

He nudges the side of my foot with his.

"We were hoping to check out early," I say.

The smile disappears from Ms. Renaurd's face. "Oh, well, sure. Of course. But you'll have an awful time getting out today. All the roads are closed for the Winter Solstice Festival."

No.

How can they close down the whole town?

CHAPTER 11

"What if there's an emergency?" I ask, my heart beating faster at even the thought of it.

Ms. Renaurd laughs. Actually, it's more of a cackle. "Oh please. Nothing ever happens around here. Everyone comes here *for the festival,* so there's no need to leave during it."

"When do the roads open?" Kyle asks, his voice sweet as sugar.

"Well, the festival goes until Christmas. But you can get your car out at night. It closes up around eleven and opens up again around eight the next morning."

I sigh, and both Kyle and Ms. Renaurd look at me.

Kyle puts a hand on my back and rubs small circles. He says to Ms. Renaurd, "Mind if we take a seat for breakfast?"

"I can see what we have left in the kitchen. Right over there is good." She points to an open table by the window.

Trudging over, I slump in the chair. Ms. Renaurd pours us each a cup of coffee, and Kyle gives her an emphatic thank-you. She gives him a million-dollar smile before heading off.

I take a sip of my coffee. It's rich and warm.

"Look," Kyle says. "We don't have the next room until tomorrow, anyway. Let's just spend the day here. We'll leave first thing in the morning and track down—who is it now?"

"Nick Thompson."

"Ah, Nick."

"That's right. You two were friends. Do you stay in touch?"

"*Were* being the operative word there." He pours some cream into his coffee, the white swirl mixing with the brown. "If he's anything like he was, he won't be hard to find."

Kyle's tone is hostile. It's so unlike him. He's usually the *friends-with-everyone* kind of guy. And if he's your good friend, then it's for life. I know what went down with Nick and me to end things, but I have no idea what happened with him and Kyle. "Why don't you like Nick? You like everyone. You even like Hank, and no one likes Hank."

"Hank is misunderstood. He's lonely."

Hank is our crankiest patron of The Vern. Misunderstood doesn't quite cover it. "And mouthy, and surly, and handsy."

Kyle places both hands on the tables, his sleeves rolled up to his elbows, showing off his impressive forearms, right now flexed and ready for a fight. "Has he still been—"

I put my hand on top of Kyle's, his skin warm under my palm. "It was just the once, honestly."

His arms relax.

"What's your deal with Nick?" I ask again.

"Who remembers after this long? I was glad when you two were through, that's for sure."

I search back. I do remember Kyle saying a couple times he couldn't figure out what I saw in Nick. Heather thought Kyle was jealous. I thought he was being protective.

Kyle goes on, "Really, I don't know him anymore. It's been how many years since he moved?"

"Four."

"Well, people change." He takes a large sip of his coffee, sets it down, and slaps his lap. "So, we good with the new plan?"

He's changing the subject. This road leads to me talking about what happened with Nick and me too, so I'm going to let it go.

"Seems like it's the only option. But what are we going to do?"

Ms. Renaurd sets a plate in front of Kyle and then one in front of me. It smells so good, I nearly drool. Toast, browned to perfection and cut in triangles, perches on the side of the plate next to a mountain of golden scrambled eggs. There are three slices of crispy bacon and four silver dollar pancakes.

"This looks amazing," I say, unwrapping my fork from the light-blue napkin.

"Thanks, hon." Ms. Renaurd places a hand on Kyle's shoulder as she leaves.

Once Kyle has devoured two of his six silver dollar pancakes, he says, "We should check out the festival."

I roll my eyes.

"Come on. You're too cool for a Winter Solstice street fair?"

"Yes. And I thought you were too."

"Nope." He snaps off a bite of bacon. "I'm all about it."

Chewing a bite of butter, maple syrup, and the fluffiest pancake I've ever had, I soften. "Fine. Let's go."

AFTER WE'VE STUFFED our faces, we grab our coats and head down the street. The air is cold and filled with delightful smells. Gingerbread, cinnamon, sugar, and underneath it all is the familiar tang of the ocean.

"Which way should we go?" Kyle's gaze roams one way and then the other.

I shrug, shoving my hands into my pockets and hiking my shoulders up to my ears.

Heading to the left, we weave past couples and families. The streets are so full, everyone smiling and chattering away. There are lights strung across the street from stand to stand, making an archway, with a golden sparkling angel in the middle every few feet.

We pass a booth selling 3D printed snowmen, reindeer and, for some reason, dragons wearing little Santa hats. The next thing that catches my eye is a stand filled with exquisite hand-knitted hats. There's a mirror hanging from the little rafter, so I try on a red one. It's ridiculously soft and slouchy enough that it actually looks nice on my mass of curls.

Kyle's face is reflected in the mirror behind me. "You look good in red."

I tilt my head to the side, taking in the image of Kyle and me together as much as the hat. My golden hair next to his dark hair. My blue eyes next to his brown. We look *good*. Kyle catches my eye in the mirror, and my cheeks flood with color, as if he could read my mind.

"You need it," Kyle declares and moves to the woman sitting on a wooden stool. "How much for the hat?"

"Twenty or two for thirty-five."

He hands over a bill.

"Kyle—"

"Thank you," he says to the woman as he links his arm with mine and pulls me away.

"You did not need to buy me a hat."

"Ah, but I *wanted* to buy you a hat. Are you warmer?"

I check in with my body. My hands aren't even in my pockets, and I am.

"Thank you," I say.

"You're welcome."

We stroll down the road, our arms still intertwined.

"Do you think you'll ever be this good?" I ask, pointing to my hat.

Kyle leans in, his face so close to mine I can feel his breath on my ear. He pulls away, and I will my heart to beat at a reasonable pace.

"No," he says.

"I was just kidding." I nudge him. "I'm sure you will eventually."

"Maybe," Kyle says, his eyes focused on a booth of handmade candles. "That's not why I do it. It's not really about *what* I make. It's the making of it that matters, if that makes any sense."

I nod, thinking of all the cookies I hastily left on my kitchen counter to get stale.

Kyle goes on. "It's cool if I make something good enough to give as a gift or something—"

"Who is getting these gifts? Where is my scarf?"

He laughs. "I didn't think you'd want one. I'm getting better, but they're not pretty. It's nice, though, to feel obligated to be good at it. I do it because I enjoy doing it. Even if I suck."

It makes perfect sense. I try to think of something I've been brave enough to do, something so new I may suck. My grandma taught me to bake when I was four years old. I'm excellent at it. I'm a damn good bartender, too. I can't think of one new thing I've tried in the past five years, in fact. Not since Grandma passed. "I never push myself to do new things."

"What are you talking about?" Kyle smiles. "You're always going to new places, to the latest restaurant two towns over."

"Yeah. I'm excellent at eating. I'll try a new place any day of the week. I know what to expect, you know? But trying a new skill like that…letting yourself suck?"

"You sucked at line dancing."

I bark out a laugh. "I did not."

His smile is devilish, his dimples popping. "You didn't. At all. You didn't know that when you tried, though."

I let that sink in. I tried something new, something scary, something I publicly could've sucked at.

"You're right. Maybe this whole unhinged adventure is good for me."

Kyle nods. "I'd say so."

"And now look at me. I'm a woman who wears hats."

"Watch out, world. She bakes, she line dances, and now she wears hats."

We both laugh, making our way down the street as we take in all the sights and smells.

THE TOWN SQUARE, which was empty and dark last night, is now filled with twinkling lights and a small stage in the middle, where a children's choir is singing "Carol of the Bells." All around the edges are tables covered in oversized gingerbread houses in every theme you can imagine.

There's a gingerbread police station, a gingerbread zoo, and even a gingerbread Disneyland castle, complete with a teeny tiny Tinker Bell. We wander past all of them.

Leaning in, Kyle points at a stand. "Want one?"

I look closer. The sign reads mulled wine. "Yes, please."

"Be right back."

Why did I think I was too cool for a street fair? This is honestly the most fun I've had in…so long I can't even remember. I find a gingerbread Airstream trailer, complete with a Christmas tree on top and a candy cane hitch. Leaning in closer, trying to figure out how they curved the dough and baked it without it breaking, I'm startled by a hand on the small of my back.

Kyle passes me my wine. "Here you are."

The cup is steaming and smells of warm, inviting spices—cinnamon, clove, and orange. I take a sip, and it's heavenly. "Yum."

"Mmm hmm." Kyle points to the gingerbread Airstream. "You ever thought of making something like that?"

I consider it. "I've made a gingerbread barn before, but it had an A-frame roof. I've never tried something curved like this."

"Have you ever thought of doing *anything* with your baking?"

I purse my lips to the side, once again thinking of the discarded cookies in the kitchen. Good thing it's not summer, or I'd come home to thousands of new six-legged roommates. "I looked into maybe setting up a booth at the farmers market, but I don't know…"

We walk toward the next gingerbread house, this one a little library with tiny gingerbread books.

"You should. People love your stuff, and you can't keep bringing it to the bar." Kyle pats his completely flat belly, which I now know after shirtless yoga is basically all muscle.

"Yeah, right." I laugh.

We find seats in the chairs set up in front of the stage. The children are now singing "Ding Dong! Merrily on High."

Kyle nudges me. "I'm serious, though. You're too good a baker not to share it."

I shrug. "What's the point? We're all just going to die someday anyway. So, what does it really matter if I do anything with my baking or let it rot in my kitchen?"

Kyle turns toward me in his chair. "That's exactly the point. Because we're all going to die. We should be doing what we're passionate about. We should be chasing our dreams. Not just pulling beers for the same people day in and day out."

Kyle's cheeks are pink—from the wine or the speech, I'm not sure.

"What about you? You gave up on real estate."

He sits back. "That was different. And I didn't give up. Just…when Mitch left me the place…" He shakes his head. "I haven't had time."

"I don't have time either."

"Bullshit."

"Oh, okay, *Poker Face*."

"You know I'm right." He turns back toward me. "I think you're scared."

I sit bolt upright. I'm a lot of things, but scared? "No. What have I ever been scared of before?"

"You just said it yourself that you don't try new things."

"Not because I'm scared. Because I'm lazy. And like I said, *what's the point*? When that giant spider crawled out from under the jukebox, who put it outside?" I point at my chest. "And when we had the slasher movie marathon, who didn't cover up their eyes?" I point again to myself. "Who has confronted not one, but two ex-boyfriends now?"

Kyle points to me.

The children stop singing, and the host of the show comes out on stage dressed in a full-on Santa suit, with such a long, scruffy beard that it must be real. Red velvet suit, black leather boots. "Next up is our lip-sync battle. There are still some spots open. If you want to show your stuff, come on up."

I grab Kyle's hand. "Come on."
"What? No."
Narrowing my eyes, I smile. "Who's scared now?"
He laughs. "I think you're missing my point."
I tug him up. "Prove your point on stage."

CHAPTER 12

Passing a trash can on the way, we toss our empty cups in, and then we find Santa.

"We'd like to sign up."

"Wonderful!" Santa claps. He points his black leather gloved hand to a table covered in scraps of paper and two big white binders. "Find what you'd like to sing. Write your name and song on a scrap of paper and stick it in the jar. We start in ten minutes."

Santa heads off to check on some other people.

I flip through the massive binder, plastic pages moving with a satisfying swish. My stomach plummets as realization sinks in. "These are all Christmas songs."

Kyle smirks as he flips through the other binder. "Yeah. It's a Christmas show. We could do a duet?"

I point my finger. "You're worried I'm going to beat the pants off you."

"If you want my pants off, you could just ask. No violence necessary."

My cheeks flood with warmth, and my mind drifts back to Kyle's hands on my hips this morning.

I snatch a piece of paper, pushing away the thoughts and my rising panic. I write the first song that catches my eye that I'm positive I know the words to. After scrawling my name next to it, I toss it into the jar. "May the best person win."

Kyle grins, writing his selection on a scrap of paper. "I can't believe you convinced me to do this."

"I can. You'd do anything for me," I say with false bravado. Honestly, I can't believe we're doing this either.

Kyle's eyes find mine. We stare at one another for a long, charged moment.

"I would," he says, his voice low.

It sends goosebumps up my arms, and I swallow hard. "'Cause we're besties."

Kyle's shoulders sag. It's small, hardly noticeable, but I see it. "Right. Friends."

We head over to the seats in front, reserved for the performers, and oh my goodness, we are underdressed. There is a woman with bright-red hair, wearing a long velvet dress, at the end of the aisle. If she had purple gloves, she'd be a dead ringer for Jessica Rabbit. Next to her are three little girls in matching red-and-white striped sweaters. And next to them is Elvis. Honest to God Elvis, in the white suit lined with rhinestones. His hair is slicked back, even more luscious than Kyle's.

I point at him. "Jealous?"

Kyle frowns. "It's a piece."

I laugh as Santa walks out onto the stage, microphone in one hand and a jar of paper scraps in the other. The crowd seems suddenly louder, and my sweater is too tight. Santa is introducing the rules of the lip-sync battle, but all I can focus on is how many people are in the crowd. Shit. This was stupid.

Santa's still talking, and the crowd erupts into applause.

Kyle nudges my arm and whispers, "He called you."

The blood drains from my face. "What?"

"He pulled your name. Go up there."

I don't move.

Kyle puts a hand on my thigh. It's warm and strong. "You're not scared of anything, remember?"

"Right." I'm not. Except, is that true? I look out on the stage and glance at the faces of strangers behind him. Strangers I never have to see again. Yeah. I'm not scared of this.

I stand and walk up the stairs to the stage. Santa hands me the microphone, and the corners of his bushy mustache turn up. He must be smiling under that beard. He says in a low, gruff voice, "Knock 'em dead, kid."

The first notes play, and I turn around—if I'm going to do this, I'm going to really do this. I drop my hip in a dramatic swish in time to each boom boom. When Eartha Kit's voice comes on, I turn around and lip sync "Santa Baby" dramatically into the mic.

There's applause from the crowd and a whoop from Kyle so loud it startles me. I swallow my smile and slink around the stage, playing it straight. Straight sexy, if I do say so myself.

The crowd eats it up. People are clapping, some are singing along, and there are a few couples in the back dancing, twirling each other around.

As the last notes play, I stroll to the back of the stage, turning around and ending as I began.

Santa heads onto the stage, grabbing the microphone. Facing the crowd, I see everyone is on their feet, applauding, hooting, and hollering, Kyle louder than all of them. A smile takes over my face, and for some odd reason, tears form in the corners of my eyes. I curtsey and head offstage, back to my seat by Kyle.

Santa introduces Elvis next as Kyle moves to let me by to my seat. "Wow."

"Beat that," I say.

Kyle smirks. "Pretty sure you just won the whole thing."

Elvis sings "Blue Christmas" on the stage, gyrating his hips, not missing a beat, and the crowd cheers even louder. I laugh.

"I don't think so. Elvis is really good."

After his performance, the three girls are next. Apparently, they're some kind of gymnasts, because they twirl and flip, actually flip their entire bodies, all to "Christmas in Hollis."

Everyone is on their feet now, moving and clapping. Kyle does the running man next to me, and I have to clutch the stitch in my side from laughing so hard.

The girls form a human pyramid for their finale. It is honestly astounding. I can't even stand on one foot for more than thirty seconds. How can they balance like that on top of one another?

The girls hop off the stage and run into the arms of their waiting parents. All of them are smiling from ear to ear, beaming. So proud.

"Well, that was quite a performance. Let's give another hand to Santa's Little Helpers."

Everyone claps as I swipe at a tear threatening to fall. I'm not sure why this silly little lip-sync show is making me so emotional.

Santa speaks again. "Next up, we have Kyle Papadopoulos."

Kyle looks at me with terror in his eyes. "I have to follow that?"

I give his arm a squeeze. "You'll be fine. Really. Remember, it's okay to suck. You love sucking."

"I did not say I love sucking."

I push him toward the stage. "Go get 'em, tiger. Suck it up."

Before the first notes of his song play, he smooths back his hair, a move I've seen him do so often...but today, standing up there on stage, it's sexy. He catches my eye and throws me a wink. The notes of his song start, and he leans into the microphone like an old-timey crooner and lip-syncs, "I'll be Home for Christmas."

It's the Michael Bublé version, and the crowd is loving it. More couples have started dancing behind the rows of chairs, holding each other close. The sun has waned, making the spotlight on the stage brighter. Kyle's handsome face is lit up, highlighting his strong jaw and his sparkling brown eyes, a shade darker in the bright light. As nervous as he seemed before he got on stage, he's in his element now.

About halfway through the song, he hops off the stage and starts strutting his way through the crowd. He takes the hand of a woman with curly white hair and spins her. She claps and then jumps up while tugging his collar down to plant a kiss on his cheek.

A few other women practically throw themselves into his arms. Kyle is unhurried, but he clearly has a destination in mind. His eyes keep finding mine. He makes his way to me and holds his hand out, all while still lip-syncing, "You can count on me."

I take his hand, and he pulls me close, dancing me all the way onto the stage. We move like we did last night in the bar, but it's a little less structured. My skin feels charged. My low back tingles under his palm. He twirls me and whispers, "Can I dip you?"

"Yes," I say just as softly.

The last line of the song starts, and Kyle tosses the microphone to Elvis, who catches it one-handed, almost like they planned it.

Kyle's strong hand grabs mine. He pushes me back, and I follow his lead as he twirls me once, twice, three times and places my hand around his neck. He moves both his hands to my back, my skin tingling under the warmth of his touch. He sinks his arms low, bringing me with him into a dramatic dip.

The crowd erupts in applause, so loud the wooden stage beneath us seems to vibrate.

People are jumping up and down. The older woman who kissed Kyle on the cheek has her hands cupped around her mouth, yelling over the applause, "Kiss her. Kiss her!"

Kyle brings me out of the dip, and instantly, my hands go to his chest.

The crowd gets in on it, and now there's a chant going.

"Kiss her! Kiss her!"

I lose myself in Kyle's melted chocolate eyes, and my mouth just talks. I don't even know what I'm saying. "We should give the people what they want."

I can see the pulse in Kyle's neck. He licks his lips, and there's a question in his eyes.

Santa comes on stage, walking in front of us. Elvis throws him the mic. "Let's hear it for Kyle, everyone."

Kyle waves and grabs my hand, tugging me off stage. We take our seats, but Kyle doesn't let my hand go, and I don't move it either.

We hold hands all through Jessica Rabbit singing "Silver Bells" in a silky-smooth voice.

Santa holds up an envelope. "I have the winner right here." He tears it open and announces, "Santa's Little Helpers!"

Everyone applauds except for the woman with the curly white hair, who I swear boos and then yells, "Kyle was robbed."

I elbow him. "You have a fan."

He smiles, his dimple popping. "I'm starving. Want to go find some food?"

"Sure."

He still doesn't drop my hand as we get up, walking off toward the heavenly smells of roast turkey and French fries. It's not like me, really. Even in my relationships, I haven't been much of a hand holder. Not that this is a relationship beyond friends being friendly…right?

CHAPTER 13

We find the food stalls, and there's just about everything you could possibly want. Clam chowder, of course, because we're still on the coast, but there are also turkey legs, Yorkshire puddings, mince pies, and more. Kyle gets a turkey leg, while I grab a bowl of mashed potatoes. We both get another cup of mulled wine and find a table under a heat lamp. The sun has dipped below the horizon, taking what little heat the day had with it, but the sky is still a light hazy blue. The first stars are just starting to twinkle.

We watch the crowd and eat our dinner as night settles over the festival. A woman walks by us in a very sexy Santa dress—low-cut, short skirt.

Kyle kicks me under the table. "You should get one of those dresses."

I shake my head. "Maybe you should go talk to her."

He levels me with a pointed stare. "I'm saying *you* would look good in it."

A shiver runs down my spine all the way to my toes.

When we're finished eating, Kyle rubs his hands together, blowing on them. Despite my hat, I'm really cold, too.

"Should we get out of here?" I ask through chattering teeth.

Kyle points to a horse-drawn carriage pulled over near the edge of the square. "Want to catch a ride?"

Bubbles of excitement fizzle in my chest. "Yes."

After Kyle talks to the driver, he gives me a hand into the white wooden carriage. The seats are red, and there's a plaid blanket draped over one. I take a seat, my jeans sliding a bit on the leather. Kyle sits next to me and throws the blanket over our laps.

The carriage turns out of the festival and onto a small road headed toward the ocean. The waves crash, one after another, on the sand beyond.

"That was some performance," Kyle says as we head down the street at a pace not much faster than walking.

"I told you I'm not scared of anything."

Kyle's eyes are pensive as he looks out at the water. He nods and swallows, not saying a word, but his face speaks volumes.

"Come on. What?"

"It's nothing."

"Kyle, you have that look…"

"What look?"

"The look you get when you want to say something but you're being too polite. How long have we been friends? You don't need to be polite with me."

He sighs, setting his hands down on his legs and smoothing the blanket. "Sometimes, I think you do that stuff because you're scared of the normal stuff."

"What do you mean by the normal stuff?"

"Like figuring out what you want to do with your life."

His words strike a chord. Part of me knows that what he's saying is exactly right. But I push that away. "I work at the bar."

"Is that your passion? Pulling pints?"

"No, but it's a job. We can't all live our dreams. What about you?"

"We're not talking about me right now. This trip isn't about me. It's about you and this love-life list. All these guys were head over heels for you, but you didn't even see it because you don't let yourself fall for anyone."

I turn to face Kyle more head on, heat rising up my neck. "That's not true."

He shakes his head. "Maybe I'm wrong, but the way I see it, you build up these walls. You make a living, you have friends, but you don't let yourself really plan for the future."

"No one is guaranteed a future," I say, my breath catching in my throat at the last word.

Kyle puts his hand on top of mine. "I know. Trust me, I know that. My mom was only thirty-seven when she passed. In three more years, I'll be older than her."

"That's what I'm saying." I squeeze Kyle's hand. "That's why none of it really matters. Who cares if I work at a bar? Who cares if I never meet the one? Who cares if I live my dreams?"

"I think the opposite. That's why it's so important. We only have so much time. Shouldn't we spend it doing things that mean something? Sharing it with someone? I'm trying to live my dreams. I am. But I'm scared, too."

Kyle's face is pale in the twilight as the carriage bumps along, the sky slowly filling with stars.

"What are you scared of?"

Kyle places his hand lightly on my cheek, the warmth of his touch spreading like an electric current under my skin. His thumb finds the edge of my jaw. My breath comes out of my parted lips, visible in the cold night.

He leans in and places his lips on mine. In high school, I imagined this moment so many times, but in reality, it's so much better than I dreamed up. His lips are softer. The pressure firmer.

I open my mouth, and so does he. His tongue finds mine, not in a hurried way, but definitely hungry. He moves his hand down my body, settling it on my hip and squeezing.

My hand is around his neck. I bring my other one there and pull myself closer to him.

The carriage stops, and we fly apart, to opposite sides of the bench.

"Here ya are, folks."

Kyle adjusts under the blanket and then steps out, offering me his hand. I take it, and this time I'm the one who doesn't let go.

We thank the driver and then head into the inn, up the stairs, and down the hall—all without a word. The air is thick between us, like our charge has its own atmosphere.

I turn the key in the door, pulling Kyle in with me. He shuts it behind him, and I can feel the click of the lock all the way down to my toes.

Practically shoving him against the door, I lean up, planting my mouth on his. His moan sends a shiver down my spine. I take off his coat as he unzips mine, all the while kissing like our lips are inseparable.

He moves both hands to the small of my back, thumbing the edge of my jeans. That little sliver of skin-to-skin contact sets me on fire. I push into him more. Needing more. I can feel his ample bulge pushing into my hip, and *oh my,* is it ever ample.

"We should take our clothes off," I say, unbuttoning Kyle's shirt.

"Should we?" Kyle mumbles lazily into my neck as he plants a kiss on a spot that literally makes my toes curl.

"Yes," I breathe out. "Now."

I get the last button undone and open his shirt dramatically, hoping to see what I saw this morning during yoga, but he has a white tank top underneath.

I groan. "More clothes."

He puts his hand on my hips, walking me backwards toward the bunk bed. "Maybe we should talk about this first?"

"No."

"No?"

We're stopped by the wood frame of the bunk bed, the edge against my back.

"Talking is overrated. We should *kiss* about this."

He plants his lips on mine, obeying my request. When we part, I'm breathless. I tug my sweater up over my head. Unlike Kyle, I do not have an undershirt. Kyle's eyes take this in, take *me* in like a slow sip of whiskey. His gaze burns on the way down.

He places a finger under my red bra strap, fiddling with it. A guttural, animal groan comes out of him that makes my hips move forward instinctively. He moves the strap off my shoulder—not the whole way, but just enough so the top of my breast is exposed but my nipple is still tucked under the red satin.

He runs his thumb over my nipple, the smooth fabric and the pressure of his touch making my nipple painfully erect in the best way. I sigh, and he brings his lips over my bra, taking me into his mouth. I want to throw the damn bra away, but it feels too good to interrupt. I want him to rip my jeans off. I want him to turn me around and yank them down.

I need more.

"Take your pants off," I breathe out.

Kyle lets out a quick exhale. But he moves his hand from my breast. His deep-brown eyes bore into mine. "I'm worried we don't want the same thing."

"I want to sit on your cock."

He laughs, his hand finding my hip and squeezing. "Okay, so we both want that, but—"

Unable to take it anymore, I duck into the bottom bunk and scoot over, patting the bed next to me and pushing down my bra strap again.

Kyle doesn't hesitate. He dives in next to me. His hands find my hips, and I crawl on top of him, kissing him deeply. His fingers start to move to the front of my jeans, unbuttoning, and I moan into his mouth.

There's a massive crack, so loud for a moment that I think it might be an earthquake.

I shoot up, hitting my head on the bottom of the top bunk, as this mattress hits the floor, splintered wood shooting across the hardwood floor.

"Shit," I say, rubbing the back of my head.

Kyle tries to sit up a bit but is fully stuck between the collapsed mattress and me. "Are you okay?" he asks, bringing a hand to my head.

"Yeah." Gingerly, I crawl out from the wreckage and then offer Kyle a hand. He takes it, but he's too tall. So instead, dropping to his hands and knees, he crawls out.

The bottom bunk is completely busted, mattress half on the floor. There are splintered wood bits all around.

I shake my head. "That's a first."

The sight is so ridiculous that a laugh bubbles up and comes out in one large bark. I cover my mouth, but it's too late. Kyle's started in on it now, and we can't stop. We end up on the floor by the fireplace, wiping tears away.

Kyle waves his hand. "Stop laughing."

I wave right back. "No, you stop laughing."

"This isn't going to be so funny when they charge us for an antique bunk bed."

I take a deep breath, trying to stop the well of giggles, but the serious look on Kyle's face as he says bunk bed is too much. "Yes, it will be. I might frame the bill."

We both laugh at that.

After a few long minutes, our laughter dies down, and I realize I'm still only in a bra. Kyle's eyes flit to my chest and away, almost like he realized the same thing. I wonder if we should pick up where we left off. My mind has rewound back to Kyle's hands on my hips, his lips on my neck...

He gets up and finds my sweater, throwing it to me. So, I guess we're done making out. Then he pulls the mattress out of the bottom bunk. "You can take the top. I'll sleep on this."

I nod. "Okay."

"We have to leave early tomorrow while the festival is closed."

"Right."

He grabs his bag and heads for the bathroom. I put my sweater on, suddenly feeling the chill in the room, and not just the draft coming from the unlit fireplace.

CHAPTER 14

We wake up bright and early, trying to beat the opening of the festival. We're both quiet this morning. We haven't really talked much at all since Kyle came out of the bathroom last night in his sweats and headed right for bed. I washed my face, wondering what the hell was going on.

We pack up our stuff in the truck, grab two cups of coffee from the café, and hit the road. The ocean fades away in the rearview mirror as we head into the trees.

The drive should take us most of the day, with good weather. We drive for hours, the music changing from *A Charlie Brown Christmas* to *Garden State*.

Somewhere along the way, we get drive-through—some not-so-excellent burgers. I must fall asleep after that, because when I open my eyes next, there is a crick in my neck and snow is falling steadily outside.

Cat Stevens is playing softly. I turn up the radio a bit, recognizing "Trouble." Grandma loved this song. She'd knead dough and belt it out at the top of her lungs.

"Not a soundtrack?" I tease.

Kyle's eyes are fixed on the road. "It is. *Harold and Maude.*"

"Are we just saying names now? Naomi and Mitchell."

Kyle smiles, and warmth blooms in my chest. We're going to be okay.

He says, "You've never seen *Harold and Maude*? How is that possible? You love romance movies. Although it is a little out there."

"Out there?"

Kyle takes a sip of his coffee then sets it back in the cup holder. "Yeah. It's about this young kid, he must be like twenty. An adult, but barely. He's obsessed with death, and he meets this older woman, like really old—in her eighties, I think—and they fall in love."

"Whoa. Now that's a May-December romance. How silly."

Kyle tilts his head to the side. "It's not, though. It's surprisingly believable that they're soulmates."

I blow out my cheeks. "Soulmates, huh?"

His deep-brown eyes flick to me, and I can feel his gaze from the tip of my scalp all the way to the soles of my feet. "You don't think there's one perfect person out there for everyone?"

I shrug. "I feel like if I did, we wouldn't be on this road trip."

"You don't have any idea who the ring is from?"

"Nope." I fiddle with the top of my coffee cup. "I'm starting to think it's not from any of them."

"Is that possible?" Kyle asks, turning down the music.

"Yeah. I mean, I've never seen it before. So, it could've just been in the suitcase, maybe."

"Where did you get the suitcase?"

"It was my grandma's. She gave it to me when I was a kid."

Kyle frowns. "So it could be your grandmother's ring?"

"No." The ring she wore for years and years is definitely not this ring. If my memory wasn't enough, the picture proved that. If she'd had another, if someone else had proposed, wouldn't she have told me about it?

My lips feel cold. I take another sip of coffee to try to warm them up. "It's probably from Nick. Out of all the ones on the list, we got the most serious."

"As serious as you ever get."

"What's that supposed to mean?"

Kyle shifts in his seat, checking behind him as he passes a slow semi. "It's just a bit of fun. Isn't that what you always say?"

"Well, yeah. But that doesn't mean there weren't real feelings involved."

"Isn't that what this whole trip is about? Proving there wasn't? Proving to Heather or to yourself… I'm not sure that you've lived a blame-free life of casual dating."

"No." I sigh. "Well, maybe. And I wanted to try to find who the ring was from and give it back. And if I really did decimate people like Heather said, I wanted to apologize. I guess."

Kyle nods.

"Why are you mad at me? Is this about last night?"

We've headed into the mountains, and snow pelts the windshield.

"I'm not mad. But I have to focus on the road."

I sink farther into my seat.

The weather gets worse the farther up the mountain we go, until we end up in a long line of cars at a complete standstill.

"Fuck," Kyle mutters under his breath.

He unplugs his phone and switches it to AM radio. An announcement is playing.

"*…special announcement from the Washington State Department of Transportation. Stevens Pass is currently closed between Scenic (milepost 58) and the summit (milepost 64) due to hazardous conditions caused by high winds and heavy snow. Motorists are advised to use alternate routes, as there are currently no detours available through the pass. Conditions are being monitored, and the pass will be reopened as soon as it is safe to do so. Drivers are urged to check the latest WSDOT updates for real-time information. Drive safely, and be prepared for potential delays.*"

"Well, shit," Kyle says, looking behind him and backing up.

"Do you know another way?"

His hands grip the steering wheel tighter. "Nope, but if we don't turn around now, we're going to have to spend all night on this highway."

"Right."

Turning the car around, he heads the other way down the road, taking the first exit. We drive the windy streets, passing a lot of churches and some farmhouses. Some horses are out in a field with plaid blankets covering them. The truck tires skid periodically, making my stomach lurch every time.

Kyle's jaw is clenched, his hands so tight on the steering wheel I think he might break it. "We need to find somewhere to stop."

I sit up, looking out the window. The snow is falling lightly. It's beautiful, really, or it would be if we were out of this truck. Pulling out my phone, I try to check the map for any kind of lodging, but nothing will load. I throw it down onto the seat. "No service."

Kyle keeps driving down the road until I spot a brown sign that says *Logging Museum – Two Miles.* I point. "That must be in town."

We follow the signs to a street called Best Road, lined with businesses all under a concrete awning with massive light bulbs like a marquee. Coffee shop, closed. Yarn store, closed. Boot shop, closed. General store, thank the universe, open. Kyle pulls over.

General is a very accurate description of what they sell. The sparsely stocked aisles hold everything from canned soup to pool toys. Yes, pool toys in the middle of December. There's even an aisle of clothing, swimsuits right next to ski masks. The front of the store has a case filled to the brim with colorful glass pipes, large hunting knives, and ornate Zippo lighters. There's a man with gray hair peeking out of his baseball cap and thick clear glasses sitting behind the case perched on a stool watching a football game. Kyle and I approach the counter. The man doesn't look our way.

Kyle clears his throat. "Excuse me, sir. We got caught in the weather. Do you know of any place to stay nearby?"

"Motel a little ways up the road. Might be full on account of the wedding."

"Wedding?" I ask.

"Mayor's daughter's getting married tomorrow. Big shindig. I wasn't invited, but practically the whole town was, and lots of out-of-town folks."

Kyle looks at me. I shrug. We might as well give it a shot.

"I'm closing up here in a couple minutes, so if you want anything, better grab it now. The motel has a real nice hot tub. Maybe get a floaty or two. They're half off."

I grab a bottle of red wine. In the clothes aisle, I find a cute light-blue bikini with a white flower pattern and a waffle texture. It looks like it's been sitting on this shelf for the last fifty years. It's perfect.

Kyle's arms are full of snacks, a six-pack of Jubelale ale, and a few plastic packages. We check out and get in the truck, driving the way the man told us to go.

The motel is impossible to miss. Kyle pulls the truck into the parking lot, and I laugh as I look up at the massive heart-shaped sign with an arrow through it. *Valentine's.*

"It feels a little like we've slipped through a time warp," I say.

Kyle nods. "Welcome to 1973."

We walk into the lobby and set our bags by the door. The room is cozy, with a sitting area by the fireplace. Stockings hang on the mantle, and a table is covered in a red tablecloth with a Charlie Brown–like tree, a few bobbles hanging here and there.

On the wall opposite the fireplace are shelves and shelves of VHS cassette tapes, most in their cardboard sleeves, but some just hanging out, black plastic on the shelf. The woman behind the counter is reading a book with a white sand beach on the cover, her brown hair, graying at the roots, tied back in a ponytail. She doesn't look up as we approach. Instead, she holds up a finger for us to wait.

Kyle looks at me, his eyes wide. I nearly laugh but cover my mouth to stifle it, thinking coming in here giggling probably won't help our cause. I wander the room, inspecting the tapes closer. *Ghost, Dirty Dancing, Road House…* This must be the Patrick Swayze shelf.

The woman sighs, puts a nail file in the book, and sets it down. "Do you lovebirds have a reservation?"

"No," Kyle says, not correcting the lovebirds comment. "We're a bit stranded. Pass is closed. We were hoping you had a room available."

She blows out a long breath and starts tapping on the keyboard of a PC that looks straight out of my second-grade typing class. After a few clicks, she smiles brightly. "You're in luck. The honeymoon suite is available. Oh, you're going to love it. Nice big bed and a view of the hot tub."

This morning was so awkward after our apparently ill-advised make out session last night. I step back to the counter. "Is there a not-quite-so-romantic room available? Maybe one with two beds?"

"Or we'd even take two rooms," Kyle says.

My stomach twists. He says he's not pissed, but it sure feels like he is.

The woman clicks a few more buttons. "This is the last room we have."

CHAPTER 15

Pulling Kyle to the side, I whisper in his ear. "Come on. We can find another place."

"Not with the mayor's kid's wedding." He shakes his head. "It's this or the truck."

I search his face. It's the same old Kyle—same crooked nose, same warm eyes, maybe a little more tired around the edges. "Are you sure this is going to be okay?"

"It has to be." He turns and heads back to the counter. "We'll take it."

Trying not to think too hard about what *it has to be* means, I go back to looking through the VHS tapes. *Ghostbusters, Groundhog's Day, Mad Dog and Glory.* This must be the Bill Murray section.

"Every room has a VCR," the woman behind the counter calls out to me as she hands Kyle a silver key hanging from a plastic heart-shaped keychain. "Feel free to take any you'd like to watch with you. Check out is at noon. And there's a chest with towels in it by the hot tub. Don't take our good bath towels down there."

"Yes, ma'am," Kyle says, nodding. "Any chance there's anywhere around here open for a bite to eat?"

"In this?" The woman blows a raspberry. "You could try the Slammer."

"Like jail?" I mouth to Kyle, *Hard pass.*

The woman laughs. "No. It's the local bar, down the street about a block. I wouldn't send paying guests to jail. Unless you take the good towels to the hot tub. Then maybe. You're in room thirteen. Down that way. Can't miss it."

I grab two cassettes off the shelf and put them in the bag with my general store purchases.

The motel is long and flat with all the rooms in a row, an awning over the whole thing, drooping with the weight of the snow. Each door is bright red, or it was probably bright sometime in the seventies. Now it's more of a murky burgundy, darkened with years of dust and exhaust, paint peeling.

Our room is the very last one in the row. Kyle hovers the key above the lock. "You ready to see the honeymoon suite?"

I laugh. "As ready as I'll ever be."

He opens the door and steps to the side. "After you."

The honeymoon suite does not disappoint. The carpet is red throughout the whole room. I peek into the bathroom near the front door, and the red carpet continues in there as well. Red carpet, red toilet, red standing shower.

"It's like something out of one of those late-night cable pornos," I say with a laugh.

Kyle rubs a hand on the back of his neck, navigating around the ridiculously large four-poster bed. "It's like something out of *The Shining.*"

The bed, thankfully, is not red. It's a white and light-pink zigzag pattern that does look an awful lot like if the red room in *Twin Peaks* was made for Barbie. There's about a billion white fluffy pillows that make it more cozy and less David Lynchy.

Across from the bed is a rolling stand with an ancient television with actual knobs. On top of the TV is the VCR the woman at the counter mentioned.

The real showstopper of the entire honeymoon suite is the red heart-shaped tub near the sliding glass doors. I run over to it and turn the knob, half expecting nothing to happen—like it's a showpiece in Ikea—but water spouts out of the tap.

I laugh. "This is nuts."

Kyle is digging through the bag he set on the nightstand. He pulls out a beer, popping the top with his keys. He takes a long pull from the bottle, his neck covered in stubble and a small, almost unnoticeable, hickey. The sight of it sends a pulse of want through me so strong, I look away.

"You all right?" I ask, setting my stuff on the other nightstand.

Kyle lowers the bottle, wiping his mouth. "Stressful drive."

"Yeah." God, I hadn't even thought of that. Here I was, thinking he's upset about me, about us, about a few harmless kisses. But he's just stressed about the weather. "Of course. Thanks again for driving and coming on this stupid—"

He cuts me off. "What are friends for?"

The sentence hangs heavy between us, almost like you could pluck it out of the air and choke on it.

"Right." Kyle slips off his shoes and points at the sliding glass door. "I'm going to get in that hot tub."

"Really? What about food?"

He pulls a blue bag out of the paper one from the general store. "Cool Ranch Doritos."

I bark out a laugh. "No. Those can't be good. Didn't they stop making them in like 2004?"

"No. These are legit. What we need to be a little leery of, but also really excited about, are these." Kyle pulls out another bag of chips, this one a brown bag of Lays with a cup of coffee printed on the front.

I grab the bag in disbelief. "Cappuccino?"

Kyle unbuttons his shirt. "Mmm."

Scanning the bag, I finally find a date. "Kyle. The best by date is December."

"Just under the wire."

"December 2015." I set the chips down and look up to find Kyle shirtless and unzipping his fly.

"Ah shit. Doritos, it is. I have some jerky, too." He steps out of his pants, working the jeans over his muscular thighs. "You coming?"

"Yeah," I say as I look away, my cheeks burning. "I'll get my suit on."

Pulling out the wine and setting it on the nightstand, I dig a little farther to find the retro blue bikini. I take it to the bathroom, closing the door behind me.

This is fine. We can use the hot tub, and nothing needs to happen. Just because we got a little carried away last night doesn't mean anything needs to change.

After tugging the suit on, I check the mirror. It's cute. High-waisted. The girls—are we still calling them the girls?—are a bit smashed in the square bandeau-style top, but it doesn't look bad. Very revealing, though. Not sure how actually water-resistant this fabric is. It feels more absorbent than anything. I pull my mass of curls up into a messy bun and head out.

Apparently, I gave Kyle enough time to open the wine—seeing as it's a screw top and he's a bartender, that's not that surprising, but it's thoughtful of him. Which isn't surprising either. Kyle's a stand-up guy. Thoughtful, attentive, and he listens. Like *really* listens.

He hands me a glass, his boxers hanging low on his hips, revealing a very pronounced V where his hips meet his legs.

I bite my lip and tear my eyes away. "Thanks."

Motioning to me, a beer bottle hanging from his fingers, his eyes firmly planted on my chest, he says, "That's some suit."

Excitement bubbles in my chest. "I found it at the general store." I pose, holding out my hand, and twirl.

Kyle chuckles. "It's very you."

Unsure that what he said is actually a compliment, I ask, "And that's a good thing?"

"That's a very good thing," he says in a low voice that makes my heart flutter. "Let's go."

I run back to the bathroom to grab a towel, but Kyle shakes his head. "Uh-uh. That woman at the counter will have our hides if we take the good towels out to the hot tub."

"But it's freezing."

Kyle smiles. "We'll have to be quick."

He opens the sliding glass door, not even bothering with shoes, which is just insane. I slip barefoot into my boots and head out first. An absolutely arctic wind nearly knocks me off my feet. I wrap my arms around myself, careful not to spill my wine. "Shit!"

Kyle slides the door closed. "The faster we go, the faster we're out of this wind."

He hops along the concrete, which is covered in a fine layer of snow. I slip and slide a bit in my Docs. There's an iron fence with Christmas lights wrapped around it, about the size of my front yard. The hot tub comes into view inside it. It's huge for a hot tub, small for a pool, and of course, it's red.

I'm about to book it for the water when I pause at a sign on the wrought iron fence around it. I laugh and lean in to make sure I read it right and then read aloud.

"We allow lovin', romancin', and fun, but for your safety, we don't allow glass past this point."

Kyle laughs while opening the gate. "Safety first."

I hold up my glass of wine that he poured for me. "So they allow boning in the pool area, but I'm about to break the rules right now with this beverage."

Kyle clinks his beer against my glass. "You're a wild one."

Setting his drink down near the edge of the hot tub, Kyle eases in. I'm mesmerized by the ripple of his abs as they disappear one by one under the bubbling water. He sighs as he leans back, his arms spread wide on the edge of the tub. "What are you waiting for?"

What am I waiting for? Isn't that the question? I set my wineglass down near Kyle's beer and take the stairs. The water is deliciously hot, so hot it's almost painful, but in a good way.

I settle onto the seat, and my eyes flick to Kyle. He's picked up his beer, but he's not moving now. Every muscle is frozen. He's watching me. Maybe the exact same way I watched him get in. His eyes shimmer in the twinkling lights—there's an intensity to them that I haven't seen since before last night. Kyle's always been handsome, but I never knew he could also be so fucking sexy.

My whole body feels warm under his gaze, and not just from the water. He takes a swig from his bottle and sets it back down on the edge. I scoot closer, facing him, and his Adam's apple jumps in his throat. I reach my arm behind him, my heart beating fast in my chest, and find my wine where I set it. I take a long sip, but I don't move away.

When I bring the glass away from my lips, Kyle takes it from my hand, setting it back on the solid ground behind him. "Safety first."

We stare at each other for a beat, and something electric breaks open between us. Like a firework's been lit, the rope burning down, until all of a sudden, there's an explosion. Kyle grabs my hips underwater and pulls me onto his lap, and I sigh at the contact. My skin has been longing to be touched by him since last night. My mouth finds his, and it feels like sweet relief.

His hands move to my ass, his thumbs fiddling with the edge of my swimsuit. And my core aches for him. I flash back to him fiddling with my bra strap yesterday.

Tonight, I'm not going to play this game of will they or won't they.

I hook my thumbs on either side of the tight bandeau top and drag the fabric down. My breasts bounce out as the fabric slides down my waist into the water. My nipples are almost painfully hard in the cold air, and Kyle's hungry gaze is glued to my chest. He's frozen, mouth slightly parted. Oh shit. I broke him.

Taking his hand from my ass, I move it to my breast. Kyle lets out a long breath that I can feel on my neck. I tilt my head back, light snowflakes falling on my cheeks, as his hand grips my breast softly at first, then firmer.

He grunts, "You're perfect."

He's harder than he was a minute ago, and I move myself up and down over the firm ridge of him. The grunt that escapes his lips echoes in my ears. It's an animal noise, one I know I'll play over and over in my head for years to come. The water, the bubbles, the pressure on my core... I moan, and Kyle brings his mouth to my breast, taking my nipple and sucking lightly.

I grind against him more, and he moves his mouth to the other breast. He sucks lightly as I run my hand down his back. His other hand moves from my ass, around the front of my suit. His fingers slide down the front of my bikini bottom, and I tense in anticipation.

A far-off laugh ripples through the air, and Kyle tenses beneath me.

CHAPTER 16

Throwing myself around Kyle's body, I cover my chest as we both listen. I can feel his heart beating eagerly against my skin. The noises get louder, and I pull up my swim top, moving off Kyle's lap. There's a couple in matching robes—there were robes?—stumbling their way toward the hot tub.

I lean in, whispering in Kyle's ear, "Should we go to the room?"

He shifts in the water. "I have a little situation."

"From what I can tell, nothing little about it."

He laughs. "Hand me a towel?"

I get out, the water droplets on my skin threatening to freeze, and find the plastic trunk filled with red-and-white striped towels. I wrap one around myself and hand one to Kyle. He pulls himself out, the muscles in his triceps popping. He grabs the towel from me, but not before I sneak a peek at the gigantic bulge pushing at his shorts. He does an adjustment and wraps the towel around his waist just as the couple enters through the gate.

We all wave, exchanging polite greetings as Kyle and I hurry off to our room. I'm through the door first, with Kyle right behind. He slides the glass door shut and closes the curtain. The scrape of the metal rings against the brass rod makes my heart race. My stomach is in knots, my eyes focused on the muscles in Kyle's back. Is this going to be a repeat of last night, where we pretend like what happened didn't happen?

Kyle turns toward me, his chest rising and falling with his breaths. He crosses the room in two long strides and places his hands on my face, cupping it softly. He leans down, pressing his lips to mine, and I melt. I'm no longer skin, no longer bones... I am only this pulsing want. A puddle of lust.

I kiss him deeply, bringing my hands around his neck. He moves his hands to my ass, lifting me up. I wrap my legs around his torso, and he moves his lips down my neck to my chest. He takes my bikini top in his teeth and drags it down.

A yelp escapes me. It's so surprising and also the hottest thing anyone has ever done.

Kyle chuckles. "You like that move, huh?"

"Mmm hmm."

He tosses me onto the bed, and I land with a little bounce. "Wait and see what else my mouth can do."

I prop myself up on my elbows and watch as Kyle moves slowly up my body, kissing my calves before moving to my thighs. He pulls at my bikini bottoms with his teeth, dragging them down my legs. I lift a little to help before tugging them off the rest of the way, impatient for his touch. He spreads me open and sits up, one of my legs in each hand. "You're so fucking perfect."

His gaze alone is making my core clench. I lie back, running my hands along my breasts. Kyle watches. "You like to touch yourself, huh?"

"Yes," I breathe out, pinching my left nipple hard.

"Have you ever thought about me while you do?"

"Yes," I moan, because it's true. I have.

"What have you wanted me to do to you?" Kyle asks as he sets one leg down and starts to move his hand slowly up my thigh to where I want him.

"Touch me." I'm shaking, I want him so bad.

"Where?"

I move his hand to my center. "Here."

He swirls his finger slowly. "Like this?"

"Yes," I moan softly.

He places a finger right at my core. "And here."

I grind into him, moving my hips, my body begging him to enter me. "Oh God, yes."

He eases the finger inside. I cry out at the sweet relief. He moves it back out, and I want him again.

"More."

He takes a second finger and eases it in. "Where were we? When you fantasized about us?"

"At the bar."

He moves his finger in and out, and my head falls back onto the bed, heat spreading through my body to my cheeks.

"And what did I do to you at the bar?"

I moan, unable to stop my body from writhing against his fingers. "This. Harder."

He thrusts deep inside me, and I cry out, "Yes."

"Did I eat your little pussy in your fantasy?"

"Yes."

He keeps his fingers snug inside me and moves his mouth to me. Licking. Swirling. Nipping and sucking. The pressure inside me builds. He starts to move his hand, but I'm so close.

I push it farther back inside.

His eyes are almost black as he sits up, his fingers continuing to work magic. "Are you going to—"

"Yes."

He thrusts again, and it undoes me. The tension in my chest explodes, my heart beating wildly. He stops moving as I pulse around him.

When I've regained my mind, I look up at him, needing more. "Condom?"

He goes to his bag, grabbing a little foil package. I move to the end of the bed, sitting up, so when he comes back, his waistband is right in my face, his bulge massive through his boxers.

I snake my fingers under the elastic band, keeping my face close as I pull them down slowly. His cock breaks free. I smile, bringing my lips to it. Kyle's moan is delicious as I take him into my mouth slowly.

"Ruby…"

Cupping his balls, I move my mouth over him, feeling him get harder and harder with each suck.

I move my hands to his ass, taking a fistful in my hand and squeezing. He pulls me up to stand, kissing me hard. I can feel his hands moving, rolling the condom on.

Pulling back, I ask, "Have you ever thought about me?"

"More than you know."

I raise my hands, my muscles stretching, my breasts lifting, enjoying every moment of his gaze on me. "How do you want me?"

He runs a hand down from my neck to my breast, lifting then letting go. He gives it a light smack. The sharp hint of pain is surprising and delicious. He moves his hand to my hip, the other firmly on his cock, and spins me around. With the smallest push, my hands are on the bed now, my ass out. He moves his foot between my legs, spreading me wider. "I pictured you bent over the bar. This pert little ass begging for my cock."

"Yes."

"Do you want me like this?"

"Yes," I moan, loud now.

He brings his cock to my entrance and stops right at the edge. The moment of hesitation lasts so long, I worry he's having second thoughts. Is he going to stop? *Should* we stop?

"Ruby."

My need for him is so overpowering. I reach around and grab him. "Kyle, I need you to fuck me. Hard."

He thrusts, and I am filled with him. God, he is big. I stretch to fit him, and he goes deeper. It's true, I have imagined this before, but it was never like this. I could never have imagined how well he would fit inside me. How good his hands would feel as he reached for my breasts, squeezing as he thrusts.

My legs start to shake. Turning me around, he lays me gently on the bed. He gets on top, bringing my leg up. He comes to the center of me, and I moan as he slides inside, even deeper than before.

"Is this okay?" His melted chocolate eyes search my face. "Too much?"

"More," I say, pulling him toward me and burying my face in his neck, kissing his salty skin. "More."

It's too much and not enough, all at the same time.

I can feel him start to tremble. Growing even larger inside me.

It feels so good. I clench, and he cries out. "Ruby."

The feeling and the power are delicious. He lets me push him onto his back. I crawl on top of him and move up and down as he watches me. His hands are firmly on my hips, bringing me down to the base of his cock every time until stars fill my vision. I arch back, clenching around him. Then, as wave after wave crashes over me, he thrusts, moving my hips and chasing his own release. We freeze for one long moment as he calls out my name again, squeezing my hips so hard, there will probably be finger marks.

I slump onto him, and he runs a hand along my back. We lie there for a long time, my body rising and falling with his breaths. I'm not sure how much time passes.

Kyle finally whispers, tickling the shell of my ear, "Did you fall asleep?"

I sigh, rolling off him and tucking myself into his side. "Just waiting for my soul to re-enter my body."

He laughs. "Wow. That good, huh?"

"Yes."

"Careful… You'll give me a big head."

I trail my hand down his stomach. "You need it to balance out what you've got going on down there."

He tilts his face to mine and gives me a long, slow kiss that leaves no doubt that it was just as good for him.

When we part, I get up and head to the bathroom, swinging my hips a little more than strictly necessary on the way, feeling his gaze on me. When I come out, Kyle heads in, giving me a playful swat on my ass.

I pull my cozy snowman socks out of my bag and nab Kyle's discarded flannel, buttoning it up. Then I grab something off the dresser as Kyle comes out of the bathroom.

His eyes crinkle at the corners as his lips curve up. "That's a good look."

My face is as serious as I can make it, my hands behind my back. "Kyle, we need to talk."

He inhales a large breath, running a hand on the back of his neck. "I know… I—"

Quickly, before he can go on—because I'm definitely not ready for whatever he's about to say—I bring the VHS tapes from around my back. "We must decide."

Kyle's smile is back, his dimple popping. He chuckles as he walks past me, grabbing a fresh pair of boxers. "Must we? We have all night. We can watch both."

He sits on the bed. I set the tapes next to him and straddle him. His hands fly to my ass like that's where they've always longed to be.

I bring my lips close to his ear. "We might be otherwise engaged."

He growls, an honest to God growl. He squeezes two fistfuls of my ass then throws me down on the bed, fiddling with the buttons of the flannel.

I laugh. "Kyle, we need to at least eat something."

"Fine. Fine. Let's watch one of those movies and have some snacks." He looks deep into my eyes. "But I can't promise I'll make it through the whole thing."

A smile takes over my face.

"What did you get?"

I grab the tapes again and hand them to him.

"*Trapped in Paradise*. Fitting. And what?" He sits up. "*Scrooged*. This is amazing."

We pop in *Scrooged* and snack on chips, snuggling on propped-up pillows. Kyle lazily runs his hand up and down my leg. Once the chips are put away, he runs his hand a little higher each time, until his fingers move up and his hand flies away. "You aren't wearing underwear."

I smile, not taking my eyes off the screen. "Nope."

"This whole time." His hand moves back to my leg, moving up and up and up.

"This whole time."

He finds my sensitive spot and touches lightly, teasing.

I moan, and his lips find mine.

I unbutton the flannel and shrug it off one arm and am about to release the other when he increases the pressure of his hand. His other hand yanks the shirt from me. I groan as he moves his hand away.

He smiles, lifting my arms up toward one of the posts of the bed. Moving his shirt around the pole, he ties it to one wrist. "Is this okay?"

"Yes." My heart flutters in my chest as he brings my other wrist to meet it and tugs tightly. The sensation makes me ache for him. I groan.

"Is that too tight?"

"No."

"Do you like it when I tie you down?"

"God, yes."

He runs his hands down my arms and over my breasts. He moves them together and lets go. "I fucking love watching your tits bounce."

"Smack them."

"You're not the boss this time, Ruby," he growls before his mouth moves down my body, starting at my neck, traveling slowly to my breast. He takes my nipple into his mouth, soft and sweet at first, then scrapes his teeth as he pulls his mouth away. The sensation is so delicious, I cry out. He keeps moving down until he finds my center, sucking and spiraling until my legs are shaking.

He stands, takes his boxers off, and unties the flannel. He takes my hands and places them on my breasts. "You're going to squeeze these beautiful tits together."

"Yes." I squeeze.

"And I'm going to rub my cock right through the center."

He spits on his hand and rubs it up and down his cock before he places it at my chest. My core clenches as it glides through my breasts. His groan is delicious. The length of him gets harder and harder with each stroke.

"Are you ready for me?" He moves his hand to my core, placing one finger inside, finding my wetness. "I'd say so."

He brings his finger to his mouth and sucks. He ties me back up before going to get a condom.

The condom rolls on slowly as I watch. He takes my legs, one in each hand, spreading them wide, as he thrusts inside, every single muscle in his abdomen tense. God, I long to touch him, but the restraints make it impossible. And so fucking hot. But my desire for him is too much.

"Kyle!"

As if he's reading my mind, he undoes the ties with one hand, still deep inside me. I run my hand along his abdomen, which is slick with sweat.

He slows his pace, lying on the bed next to me, big spoon—and I do mean big—to my little. I back up into him, coming down hard on his cock every time. He grabs my hair and brings his mouth to my neck. The tug of his fist, the pulse of his cock… It's all too much. I cry out as one massive pulse washes over me.

He grunts as I clench around him, letting my hair go and bringing me closer to him. His stomach is slick on my back, his arms wrapped around me. Tingles course through me. We lie there, both of us shuddering in the aftermath of what we've just done.

CHAPTER 17

In the morning, bright-white light peeks through the red curtains and right onto my face. I throw the blanket over my head to block it out. I have no idea what time it is, but I know for a fact it's too early. Last night, we stayed up late. We watched both movies, in between other activities, although Kyle fell asleep at the end of *Trapped in Paradise.*

Moving my arm across the bed, I feel around for Kyle, but there's nothing but cold sheets. I throw the covers off and sit up. "Kyle?"

Nothing.

Grabbing his flannel off the floor and shrugging it on, flashes of last night coming back to me—Kyle wrapping this around my wrists —I pad to the bathroom. It's empty, too.

Checking my phone, I see that I have two texts.

Kyle: Tracking down coffee and checking the status of the pass.

That explains it. I turn on the shower and wait for the water to warm up as I read and reread the text. Not very lovey dovey. Not that we're in love. We're friends. I mean, I love him as a friend. Friends that now sleep together. More like the most intense orgasms of my life together. Once we're back home, will we still sleep together?

When I check the water, it's still freezing. I head back into the room and spot the heart-shaped tub. Turning the knob, I feel the hot water as it pours out. Bath, it is. I read the other text.

Heather: Call me.

Shit. It was sent last night at 11:08.

Sitting on the edge of the tub, I hit the video chat icon.

Heather picks up on the second ring, her eyes red and swollen, her hair pulled back with a headband.

"Oh, honey," I say, my heart sinking into my stomach. I'm going to kill him. "What happened?"

Her face crumples like a wadded up tissue. "He's still talking to her."

"What?"

"Theo. We're out here at his parents' house, and last night I caught him in the bathroom talking to that woman."

I nod. "The one from the parking lot?"

A sob rattles through her. "He loves her. He must. Why else would he still be talking to her? We're through."

"Where are you?"

"In the bathroom."

"What city, honey? Where do his parents live?"

"Cedar Valley."

I check the map on my phone, the little video screen getting smaller. It's definitely not on the way. But that's okay.

"Okay. We'll come get you."

"The road is closed."

"Right, but as soon as it isn't, we'll be there."

"Okay." She wipes a tear away and squints at the screen. "Where are you?"

"Oh, man. This place is wild." I turn the camera around and give her the tour. The red carpet, the heart tub, the massive four-poster bed, still rumpled.

"This is nuts. What's Kyle's room look like?"

I swing the phone quickly away from the rumpled bed toward the nightstand. "Um, there was only one room available…"

"Oh my God. Ruby!"

I bring the phone back to my face. "What?"

"Was that a condom wrapper on the nightstand?"

I glance over. Yep. Sure is. Well, I was going to tell Heather about it eventually. I sink onto the bed. "We slept together…four times."

"Finally. Wait, four times! Holy shit. How was it? Was it sweet? I bet Kyle is a very gentle lover."

Heat floods my cheeks at how absolutely untrue that statement is. "It was sweet, but he was *not* gentle. In the best way."

"Oooh." Heather puts a hand to her mouth. "I always knew you two—" She stops talking abruptly, clamping her mouth shut.

"You always knew what?"

She frowns, pursing her lips tighter.

"Heather!"

"I always thought you two had feelings for each other."

I sigh. "That's not what this is. We're just friends."

"That sleep together."

"Right. Fun. Easy. No mess," I say as I turn off the tap for the tub. The water is steaming.

"Like all the guys on your list, right?"

The muscles in my shoulders tighten. A fierce part of me wants to argue. It's nothing like that. Because as much as I thought I was keeping it light with all of them, it turns out—so far, anyway—that wasn't really the case. I hurt them by being aloof. By ending things abruptly. By pretending things—them…us—didn't matter.

I don't want Kyle to end up on that list. But what does that mean?

"My bath is ready. I gotta go. I'll let you know when the pass opens, and we'll swoop you up."

"Okay. Thank you. And Ruby…"

I wait with my heart in my throat, but she doesn't go on. Finally, I say, "What is it?"

She sniffles and wipes another tear away. "Be careful. Don't break his heart."

I sink into the tub, feeling like scum. Heather is right. I shouldn't have let things get out of hand with Kyle. Or we should've at least laid some ground rules. Like neither of us will fall in love with the other. But is that a rule you can really set? I've had that conversation before, and look how well that turned out. I thought I had it all figured out with Josh, with Liam, and I was wrong on both fronts. They wanted something real, and I pushed them away.

I'll tell Kyle it was a mistake. We had a slip. It happens. We'll go back to being friends—who don't kiss, who don't suck each other's…

The door to the room opens, and I cover up instinctively. A tub in the middle of the room is not really the best for modesty. Kyle walks in, a paper cup in each hand and a bag hanging from his teeth. He shuts the door with his foot. His cheeks are rosy, probably from the fresh air and the cold. He sets the cups down and then the bag. His gaze lands on me in the tub, and despite my plans to not make out with Kyle again, I move my arm away from my breasts, my nipples just peeking up above the waterline.

Kyle unbuttons his jacket, throwing it onto the floor. "Good morning."

I lean back, pushing my chest out a bit more, laying my arms on the edge of the tub and crossing my legs. "Good morning to you."

His pupils swell as he kicks off his shoes and crosses the room in two large strides. He steps into the tub in all his clothes.

I laugh. "Kyle, your clothes."

He dives for my breasts, his mouth going right for my nipple, sucking lightly at first and then nipping the tiniest bit with his teeth. Moaning, I lean my head back, laying it on the edge of the tub.

Tomorrow. We'll go back to being just friends tomorrow.

The pass is still closed. Kyle and I spend the day in bed. I grab two more movies from the lobby: *The Holiday* and *Die Hard*. But we don't make it through one before melting into each other. I can't stop kissing him. His lips are so soft, but the way he kisses is anything but.

Eventually, he gets out of bed and says, "I'm starving."

We had breakfast sandwiches this morning that he got from a nearby café, and we snacked on some beef jerky, but that's it. And we have been busy.

"Should we check out the jail bar?"

Kyle chuckles. "Let's do it."

We bundle up. The sun has already set, and the night is clear, the sky filled with stars. Kyle holds my hand as we walk down the sidewalk. If it didn't feel so good, I'd try to move away. Hand holding isn't really a friends-with-benefits activity.

The walk to the Slammer is freezing but mercifully quick. The bar is no frills, that's for sure. It's a brick building with a window with bars covering it. Not sure if it's an actual safety measure or a decoration. Above the burnt-orange door is a neon sign in the shape of an arrow that says *Bar*.

Kyle holds the door for me as we head in. Ella Fitzgerald plays over the speakers. "Have Yourself a Merry Little Christmas." My boots clack on the unfinished wood floor. The whole bar is a mass of wood. Wood bar stools with brass details, long wooden bar, round wood tables and matching chairs.

Despite the weather, or maybe because of it, the place is full. The big screen television in the back is playing a football game. People are either watching it intently or chatting, bothering the people watching it.

Kyle moves to two empty bar stools and pulls one out for me. When the bartender comes over, I order a hot toddy, and Kyle orders a Scotch ale. Kyle has an arm draped around the back of my chair, looking around the bar.

"See anything you like?" I ask, and he turns his gaze to me.

His smile is devilish. "Uh-huh."

I swat him on the shoulder. "I mean about the bar."

He shrugs, looking around again. "Their television is nicer than The Vern's."

I nod. It's true. "What are you going to do?"

"About the TV?" He smirks. He knows that's not what I mean.

I shake my head.

He sighs. "I don't know. I've just been muddling through. I had no idea Mitch was going to leave me the place."

"Yeah," I say, fiddling with the handle on my mug. "Didn't he have a son?"

Kyle takes a long pull from his beer. "He passed."

I turn my attention back to my drink. I met Mitch's son. It must've been three years ago now. He was my age. How can he have died, and why didn't Mitch say anything? "What happened?"

"Bad luck. Car accident."

"Why didn't Mitch talk about it?"

Kyle shrugs. "He was pretty private. Remember when he took all that time off last year?"

Mitch's son, gone. Mitch not long after. My grandma. Kyle's mom. Can people stop dying all the time? I slam my cup down on the bar a little harder than I mean to.

Kyle places a hand on my shoulder. "You okay?"

"Yeah." I stand. "I need to use the bathroom."

I head down the hallway marked restrooms and walk into a crowd of women leaning in toward the mirror. Lipstick gliding on. Noses being powdered. All the stalls closed. I wait off to the side, taking deep breaths and trying to calm my beating heart. Two more women crowd into the tiny space, one with bright-red hair and long red nails, the other with a freckled button nose. I move over to make room.

One of the stall doors opens, and the woman behind me practically yells, "She needs to go first. She's getting married tomorrow."

I laugh, because there is absolutely no logic to that at all. But I sweep my arms toward the stall. "Go ahead. Got to get something out of getting married, right?"

The woman with her brown hair and freckles shakes her head. "No, I can't. You were waiting."

"You can go," I say.

The woman with red hair jumps ahead of both of us. "I'm going."

The bride-to-be and I look at each other and laugh. She motions to the stall her friend went in and mimes drinking.

"Yeah," I whisper. "I could tell."

She giggles. "I swear. It seems like everyone else is more excited for this wedding than I am."

I look at her, really look at her. She's beautiful. High cheekbones. Thick hair. Deep-brown eyes, and a smattering of freckles on her nose. "Why get married, then? You're gorgeous. You don't have to tie yourself down."

"It's not. It's binding me to him, and even if we never got married, we are bound. Our souls are tangled up. He's the one for me."

"How do you know?"

"Whenever something exciting happens, he's the one I want to tell. He holds the door open for me. He puts his hand my low back when we leave the movie theater, and to this day, I get a little thrill from it. He tells me I look nice. He rubs my feet when we watch *Survivor*. It sounds silly, but it's the little things that make up a life."

"Aren't you afraid?" The question just comes out. Because isn't that the rub of the whole thing? If you let yourself love someone completely, when you lose them—and eventually you will, be it to cheating, or petty arguments, or cancer. Nothing and no one lasts forever. When that happens, you will be completely destroyed.

"I am. But I love him more than that. More than the fear of what might happen." She turns to me and sighs. "It's all the wedding stuff that's a drag. If I could, I'd run out right now and get married without all the hoopla. Me and him and the stars."

Her friend comes out of the stall. As I go in, an idea comes to me. I remember my friend Meg's wedding last year. When I come out of the bathroom, I grab the bride's arm. "Is your fiancé here?"

She nods. "Yeah, watching the game."

I lower my voice. "If you're serious about the whole you, him, and the stars, I might have an idea."

CHAPTER 18

Rushing to Kyle's side, I grab his arm. "Hey, are you still ordained?"

Kyle's eyes narrow. "Yes."

The apprehension in his voice is so palpable, I laugh.

"Come on. I need your help." I tug his arm and practically drag him out to the back patio the bride told me about.

There's a poinsettia on one of the little round tables, and I grab it on impulse.

"Ruby, where are we going?" Kyle asks, moving his hand down to mine and squeezing it.

I open the door to the empty patio. Gravel crunches under my feet, and there's my new friend, who I'm just now realizing I have no idea what her name is. She's standing there holding hands with a tall man with sandy-blond hair and a beard to match. I pluck one of the poinsettias off and hand it to her.

I take Kyle by the arms, guiding him to stand between them. "Kyle, this is…"

"Lisa," the bride says helpfully. She lifts her man's hand up. "And Chris."

I smile. "Lisa and Chris would like to get married."

Kyle's eyes go wide. "What? Now? They need paperwork and…"

Lisa jumps in. "We have all that. We're having a big wedding tomorrow. But we want something for us."

Kyle's eyes find mine, and I smile. He nods and looks back at the couple. "Okay… Dearly beloved…"

ONCE THE CEREMONY IS DONE, we leave the newlyweds to bask in being married and head back inside. As we navigate through the crowd of people, Kyle puts a hand on the small of my back, and I feel it all the way to my heart.

"Do you want another drink?" he asks.

"No." I turn, placing my arms around his neck, lifting on tiptoes to reach his lips.

He leans down, closing the distance between us, and kisses me. It's soft and sweet, and it feels full of promises we have yet to make.

We gather our things and head out into the night.

"That was unexpected," Kyle says, putting his hands in his pockets.

"It was. I remembered you did Meg and Tommy's," I say, thinking of the dreamy look on the bride's face. They're really in love. "Hope you don't mind I offered your services."

"Yeah—no. It's cool. You surprised me. It's so *romantic.*"

My mouth falls open. "I can be romantic."

Kyle holds up both hands. "Okay. I've never seen that side of you. Whenever you talked about Nick, you were always so…" He trails off.

I think back to Kyle asking me how things were going, or even Heather, how I deflected with my old standby. *It's fun, for now.*

For now. I would actually say that. Even when things were going really well with Nick and me, I never let it permeate my skin. It could never become something serious, because I would never let it. God, I am cold. But I've had to be.

"So?" I ask, my hackles up.

"Nah," Kyle says. "It was nice, that's all I'm saying."

"But what are you *not* saying?"

He blows out a long breath. "Okay, don't take this the wrong way, but you always seemed a little cynical about love before."

It hits me right in the center of my chest, and not because it's wrong. *Cynical.*

Kyle goes on. "Like if that wedding had happened at The Vern, you would've rolled your eyes so hard, I would've had to pick you up off the floor. You definitely wouldn't have orchestrated it."

"Yeah…" I hop over a large crack in the sidewalk. "You're not wrong."

He licks his lips. "What changed?"

I'm not sure anything really has. Isn't that what this whole mission is about, proving that relationships can be just fun—no strings, no souls intertwined and then destroyed? That there can be no hard feelings? Except Liam had more feelings about it than I expected.

Kyle's waiting for my answer.

I shrug. "Nothing's changed. I'm in a good mood, that's all." I lower my voice, leaning in. "I got laid."

Something in Kyle's eyes shifts for a moment. It's there and gone so fast, I wonder if I imagined it. He smiles. "Right."

When we get to our room, Kyle uses the bathroom. I want to shake off the heavy feeling I have after our conversation. Pouring myself a glass of wine, I step out of my shoes and shimmy out of my pants.

Nothing like a little seduction to push the bad feelings away.

Hmm. I did not pack any fancy lingerie on this trip. The sink turns on in the bathroom. I have to act fast. I lose the rest of my clothes, stripping down to my black thong. Grabbing the velvet ribbon off the curtains, I wrap it around myself. I can just barely tie it into a large bow around my breasts. Then I perch on the dresser, crossing my legs, and wait.

And wait. And wait.

The water is still running. Is he taking a shower? In the cold water?

I bring my wine over to my perch on the dresser, sipping and thinking. Maybe Kyle and I should talk about what we're doing here. What if he was hoping this was going to turn into something more? I hear the water turn off and set my wine down, returning to my carefully crafted pose. We can talk tomorrow. I am wrapped up, after all.

Kyle comes out of the bathroom, dripping wet in nothing but a towel. He freezes when he sees me, bringing a hand to his growing smile.

"Oh my," he says.

In my breathiest Mr. President voice, I say, "Merry Christmas."

"Christmas isn't for a few days."

"Happy Hanukkah?"

"You're not Jewish." He crosses the space between us and fiddles with the edge of the ribbon. "And I'm pretty sure this isn't kosher."

I run a finger down his wet abs to his towel and tug. It falls to the floor, and my core clenches at the sight of him.

"Mmm. Merry Christmas to me," I say as I run a hand along his length, feeling him grow under my palm. His hands move to my thighs, and he squeezes. I give him one long, firm stroke and hop off the dresser. Walking around him and leaning against one of the posters of the bed, I raise my arms as he watches me. Bringing my hands slowly down, I run them along my breasts, keeping the ribbon, down my stomach, and to my thong, grabbing the straps. I turn around, giving him a front-row view of my ass as I bend over, taking the thong off completely.

Kyle grunts but doesn't move toward me yet. His gaze is intoxicating. I grab the bedpost with one hand and bring the other to my swollen rosebud slit and swirl, moaning at how good it feels to have him watch me do this.

"Fuck, Ruby," Kyle grits out.

I turn to wink over my shoulder. "You wish."

He crosses the room, cock in his hand, and brings his other hand to my hip. I grab the bedpost with both hands as he rubs his cock on my ass. He brings his hands to the ribbon and unties the knot. My breasts fall, leaving my nipples hard, aching for his touch.

Bringing my hands close together at the bedpost, I whisper, "Tie me up."

He chuckles. "For a girl who doesn't like to be tied down, you sure like to be tied up."

I'm too worked up to unpack that statement. I need him. "Please, Kyle."

He takes the ribbon and ties it around my wrists, fastening it to the wooden post. Moving his hands to my hips, he bends me over a bit more. He runs his hand along my ass gently. "Tell me what you want."

"Smack my ass."

He brings his hand down in a swift motion and gives my ass a firm smack. The shock of it sends a pulse of want straight between my thighs. Apparently, you don't have to ask him twice.

"Again," I say.

He brings the other hand to the other cheek, but after the smack, he leaves it there and squeezes, tugging my ass against his hard cock. One hand moves to my clit, and he swirls while the other keeps me firmly against him as he begins to grind against me.

"Fuck me," I breathe out.

"What was that?" Kyle asks, his swirling increasing in pressure.

"Fuck me. Oh God. Please, Kyle."

He leaves and is back in a moment. If my hands weren't tied, I would've continued the motion of his fingers. The satisfying shriek of foil of the wrapper sends goosebumps up my arms. It falls at my feet a moment later.

Taking my hips in his hands, he lines us up. He's so hard. He stays there, snug against my entrance, but doesn't move, teasing me.

"Kyle..." I whine.

He moves one of his hands off my hip and brings it to my breast. Taking my nipple between his thumb and pointer finger, he squeezes tightly as he thrusts slowly inside me, filling me inch by inch. I cry out.

"Too much?"

"More."

He grunts and brings his other hand to the other nipple. Sliding his cock almost all the way out, he squeezes both nipples as he thrusts, still deliciously slow. My thighs tremble.

"Do you want to move to the bed?"

"No. More."

He cups my breasts as he increases the pace, thrusting over and over, filling me. I moan out his name. All other thoughts are lost in the sensation.

Kyle reaches up and unties the ribbon. Turning me around, he kisses me. Then he lifts me up, leaning my back against the wall, still holding me in the air as he thrusts over and over. The wall is cold and hard on my back.

"Oh God," I breathe. "Kyle, I'm close."

"Let that sweet little pussy go."

"Oh, fuck."

He swells as I clench. The world freezes, and his gaze locks on mine. My heart riots, beating impossibly fast as I let go, crying out his name. His arms are shaking. He lays his forehead on my shoulder as he releases too. After a moment, he carries me to the bed, laying me down and then snuggling up next to me. We lie together, our chests rising and falling, both a sweaty, happy mess.

It's still dark outside when Kyle wakes me up with a gentle kiss.

"Mmm."

"The pass is open. We should get going if we're stopping to get Heather."

Heather. Shit. That wakes me up. I send her a text that we're on the way.

When I get out of bed, we pack up our things. Mercifully, the café is open, so we're able to grab coffees before getting on the road. Kyle plugs in his phone, and music fills the car. I recognize it—Karen O's "Moon Song."

"What movie is this from?" I ask, cupping my hands around the coffee, wishing it was a blanket I could wrap around myself.

"*Her*," Kyle says.

"Right. I forgot about that one."

A light snow is falling, and in the dark it looks like we're moving through stars. The snow, the ethereal music, warm coffee, Kyle. It's dreamy.

I settle back in my seat and take it all in. "What was *Her* even about?"

Kyle answers immediately, like he's already given this a lot of thought. "It's about finding love in unexpected places."

"It is?"

Kyle smiles, his dimple popping. "Maybe. I only saw it once. It's a great soundtrack, though."

I tap the icon for the internet, and for once, it actually loads the page. "Reddit says it's about the emancipation of women from the patriarchy."

Kyle nods, grabbing his coffee cup from the center console. "Huh. Yeah, okay. I can see that. Fuck the patriarchy."

I tap my paper cup to his. "Cheers to that."

"I might need to rewatch it." Kyle's face, with its strong planes, is lit by the dashboard controls.

"These soundtracks aren't all from your favorite movies?"

He shakes his head.

"So what's with them, then? Why all the soundtracks?"

"My mom used to listen to them all the time. Her favorite was *Little Women*—the Winona Ryder one. It's on here if you want to listen."

"Sure." I pick up his phone and find the soundtrack.

Kyle gets quiet, his eyes focused on the road, and we both listen. A tear falls onto his lap, soaking into his jeans. I place my hand over the spot.

He wipes his face. "It'll be twenty years this Christmas."

I squeeze his thigh but don't offer any condolences. I know they don't help.

Inhaling a shaky breath, he places his hand on mine. "Sometimes, it just sneaks up on you. You know?"

"I do." My grandma's only been gone five years. Some days, I'm fine. Some, I feel her absence like a hole in my pants, a cool breeze seeping through. And some it's like I'm naked in the snow. I will never be warm again. Nothing will ever be right.

"Listening to soundtracks, even if it's ones she never heard..." He shrugs. "I feel closer to her."

"I feel the same way when I bake. Like my grandma's right there with me."

We drive without stopping, listening to beautiful music, my hand resting lightly on Kyle's thigh. The sun comes up over the mountain, bathing the road in a golden light, and my hand remains. I'm not usually a casually affectionate person with someone I'm sleeping with. Either we're making out and touching all over, or we're not. Maybe it's because Kyle and I were already so close. Already casually affectionate. Whatever the reason, it's new, and I definitely don't hate it.

CHAPTER 19

As we exit the freeway and wind down back roads, we pass a lake, the water ice blue and reflecting the gray clouds above. It's so still, not a ripple. There's a rest stop up ahead, and I point. "Restroom?"

Kyle nods and pulls off.

When I come out of the bathroom, Kyle is standing at the viewpoint, his hands resting lightly on the stone wall. I stand next to him, and he points. Off in the distance, there is a huge nest way up in a tree. It has to be wider than Kyle is tall, and Kyle's a tall dude.

"Whoa. It's gigantic."

Kyle chuckles. "That's what she said."

I nudge him with my shoulder, and he puts his arm around me, pulling me in close.

We watch as an eagle circles overhead and lands in the nest.

"It's amazing they can build that," I say.

Kyle nods. "It's because they mate for life."

"What?" I look up into his eyes.

He's smiling, his dimple popping.

"You're fucking with me. That is not why."

"No, I'm serious." Kyle pulls me in closer, bringing his hands to the small of my back. I wrap my arms around his neck. "I read that the reason eagles can build such enormous nests is because they have a partner they trust, that will always be there. And they work on it together. Little by little. Stick by stick. They can add to it over the years."

Kyle's eyes are warm as his hands move down, resting gently on my ass. A gust of wind blows my hair back.

"What if it gets knocked down?"

He leans down. "They rebuild."

He brings his lips to mine. The wind blows on my fingertips. There's a soft smell in the air. That indescribable scent that comes right before it snows. It mingles with Kyle's woodsmoke-wool musk, and the mixture is heady. Our kiss lingers. It's hot, but there's something else to it, something sweet. There's a pulse low in my belly, but there's also a stirring in my heart. This kiss isn't just hot. This kiss feels like home.

I pull back abruptly, my heart beating ferociously. "We should get to Heather."

Kyle nods, his eyes searching my face. "Ruby, we need to talk about us."

Walking back to the truck, I say, "No, we really don't." I climb in and buckle my seat belt.

Kyle does the same, but he turns in his seat to face me. "I'd like to talk about it."

I snuggle into the side of my seat, leaning against the window. "Kyle, we're friends who got carried away and fucked. Nothing to talk about. Happens to the best of us. It's like *When Harry Met Sally*... Men and women can never just be friends, because sex always gets in the way. It happens. We'll get it out of our system, and by the time we're back home, everything will go back to normal."

Kyle's jaw is clenched, his eyes still searching my face. "Is that what you want? For things to go back to normal?"

I sigh dramatically. Mostly to cover the lurch in my stomach at the thought of not kissing Kyle anymore, not sleeping with him, not casually touching him. Why does that bother me so much?

"I do." I don't. "Desperately." I desperately want his hand back on my thigh. "Can we get on the road? Heather is waiting."

Although I haven't heard back from her…

He starts the engine and pulls out, his eyes solely focused on the road.

AROUND MIDDAY, we pull up to the house Heather gave me the address of.

"Think we can use their bathroom?" Kyle asks.

I frown. "Maybe."

We both get out, trudging through about four inches of snow to the stately house. The place is huge and has actual columns holding up the wraparound porch. It looks like a house you'd see in a movie set in the South more than something two hours outside Leavenworth, Washington, in basically the middle of nowhere.

I hesitate, wondering if I should knock or send Heather a text, when the door flies open and a little girl with blonde pigtails flashes me a bright, somewhat toothless smile.

"Did Santa send you?" she asks, her eyes hopeful.

"No, I'm here to pick up my friend Heather."

The little girl goes back inside, leaving the door hanging open.

"Should we go in?" I ask.

Kyle peeks inside, spotting an open door to a bathroom off the entryway. "I'm going in."

He books it to the little room, shutting the door, so I step in as well. Getting out my phone, I send Heather a text.

A blonde woman in a cream sweater comes down the stairs and freezes at the top step when she sees me. "Excuse me?"

I hold up both hands. "The little girl let me in. I'm here to pick up Heather."

Kyle comes out of the bathroom, striding over to stand next to me.

The woman's eyes go wide, her hand flying to her chest. "I see you've made yourselves at home."

"Sorry, ma'am," Kyle says. "It was an emergency."

She waves her hand toward the living room. "Go sit in there. I'll find her."

The woman heads back up the stairs, and we enter the living room. There's a massive tree in the corner decorated with equally massive red and green bobbles.

Kyle takes a seat on the beige couch, and I sit next to him.

"I should've texted," I whisper.

We hear yelling from upstairs, and Kyle's gaze moves toward the entryway. "Yep. Probably. Maybe I should wait in the car?"

"Don't you dare leave me," I say, grabbing his arm.

He slips his hand into mine, and relief spreads over me. The rest of the ride here, he kept his hands firmly on the wheel. I was worried our touching phase was over after what I'd said at the rest stop.

"It was a joke," he says, his voice low. "I'd never leave you."

Warmth spreads in my chest at those words.

Heather comes down the stairs in a fuzzy robe and slippers. Absolutely not ready to go.

Frowning, I say, "You're not ready?"

Heather looks pointedly at my hand holding Kyle's, then she locks eyes with me, raising her eyebrows. A silent question.

I drop Kyle's hand. "Do you need a hand getting your things?"

She crosses her arms. "I'm not going."

"What?" I cross the room, and we move to the entryway.

"You didn't get my text?"

I pull out my phone. I hold up our text thread to show her. There's nothing.

"I sent you one, I swear," Heather says, grabbing her own phone out of her robe pocket. Her face falls. "Shit. I didn't hit send." She taps the screen. "There. Sorry."

I look at my phone.

Heather: I'm not leaving. Theo and I made up. We're going to give it another shot. Love you.

"What do you mean, you made up? He's sleeping with someone else."

Her shoulders sag at my words. "He was confused before."

"Was he confused when that other woman's mouth was on his dick?"

Heather pulls me out onto the porch.

Kyle moves past us, squeezing my shoulder. "I'll be right over there if you need me." He points toward the truck, and I nod.

Heather makes eyes at me. She whispers, "What's with all the touching? I thought you were just friends."

"We are," I say, shooting daggers at her. She is not going to turn this into a discussion about Kyle and me.

"You told me you slept together—you didn't mention the *hand holding*." She points to the flannel tied around my waist. Kyle's flannel. "Is that his shirt?"

"We're not talking about that right now."

Heather crosses her arms. "Oh yes, we are."

I lift my arms. I give up. "Yes. We've been holding hands. And resting our hands on each other's legs. And sometimes he puts his hand on the small of my back, and it drives me wild. Absolutely feral. Now go get your stuff. If you want to forgive Theo, fine. Do it in Fortune Falls."

She sighs. "Thank you for coming here. I'm sorry I fucked up the text. But I'm good here. He was talking to her because she had left a sweater at his house from before. When they were… But they're not now. It really is over between them. He loves me."

Left something at his house. Yeah, fucking right. I plant my boots firmly on the porch. "I'm not leaving you here."

Theo comes out of the house, wrapping an arm around Heather's shoulders. "Hey, Ruby. I didn't know you were stopping by. Kind of a trek, huh?"

"She's headed to Leavenworth," Heather says.

"Ah." He pulls Heather in closer. "That's a ways off."

I smile. "Yeah. Heather's coming, too. She was about to go grab her stuff."

Theo's brow furrows.

"She's kidding." Heather shoots me a death glare. "They stopped by to wish us Happy Holidays."

"You could've just called." He chuckles.

"Ruby is very into face-to-face communication."

"Mom put lunch on—do you want to come in?" he asks with a smile so slick that if I stare at it for too long, I'll slip.

"No," I say a little harsher than I mean to, but I'm so mad. How can Heather go back to this smarmy asshole? He's so fake, with his car salesman smile and his firm grip on Heather's shoulders. There's no way that woman left her sweater at his house.

"Thanks for the offer," I say a bit softer. Because if they're back together, I don't want to lose my friend by alienating her boyfriend. "We should get on the road."

I mouth *Call me* to Heather. She pulls me into a swift hug. I squeeze her back and wonder if I could pick her up and run. But she's much taller than I am, so probably not.

"Thank you for coming out here," she says into my hair, currently a wild mass of curls I haven't done anything with all day.

"Text me."

I head back to the truck and climb in.

Kyle starts the engine. "Heather getting her stuff?"

I shake my head.

"Ahh, I see." He pulls away from the house. "You okay?"

I shrug. I am. I can't make Heather's decisions for her, but God, I really wish I could. "Yeah."

He smiles. "Leavenworth, here we come."

Should we even go? The whole thing seems stupid now. What does it matter if Nick's version of events is different from mine? What does it even matter if he was going to propose? We were together, and now we're not.

End of.

"I don't know. Maybe we should head home." I cross my arms, feeling the chill of the car in my bones.

Kyle places his hand on my thigh. "I have to stop at least for the night and see my sister."

Fuck. Right. He told me that at the beginning of the trip.

"You remember Chloe? Maybe not. She's quite a bit younger. But you two should hang. I think you'd really hit it off."

"Oh...um..." First all this casual touching, then he wants to talk about us, and now I'm meeting his family. This doesn't feel like friends with benefits. I have to stop this before anyone gets hurt. "No, I don't want to intrude."

He squeezes my thigh. "It's not intruding. I'm inviting you."

I shift in my seat, moving my legs to the side. Kyle's hand finds the steering wheel again. Tapping some things on my phone screen, I show it to Kyle. "The reservation goes through tonight. So, there should be a room. You can drop me off in town."

He nods, but the corner of his mouth sags. I lean against the window and close my eyes tight, trying to sleep or at least to pretend to.

ONCE WE'RE a little outside Leavenworth, Kyle turns down the music. "Do you want to talk about it?"

"No," I say.

He licks his lips. God, it's so sexy. Why is everything he does so sexy now? The way the veins in his hands pop as he grips the steering wheel. The way his forearms flex as he passes a slow car. The way the gray winter light hits his jawline. I had a crush on Kyle before, but this is ridiculous.

"If you do, I'm here." He reaches over, turning the music back up.

The sun is waning by the time we pull into downtown Leavenworth. The cream houses are covered in dark-wood trim in a Bavarian style more fitting of a German village than a Washington mountain town. But it's charming. Lights and garlands hang from every available surface. The large mountain serves as the backdrop for the quaint street.

Kyle pulls over in front of the Icicle Lodge and turns the car off.

"Are you sure you don't want to come to my sister's? She's making lasagna."

Mmm. After gas station snacks all day, homemade food sounds amazing. I sort of remember Chloe. She was a few years younger. Usually off riding her bike with a doll hanging off the front when I'd come over. His other sister is older, so by the time we started hanging out, she was away at college. But this thing between Kyle and me has gone far enough. If I go with him, it'll be sending the wrong message. "No, I can't go. No family. But if you want to stay longer than today, I can totally get the train back home from here."

"What are you talking about, *no family*? You've been to my dad's a billion times. Oh…" Heavy lines appear around his mouth, and he looks like I just punched him in the face. "This is because—"

I can't stand the hurt in his eyes.

"It's because we've been fucking. And you want to talk about"—I hold up my fingers in air quotes—"*us*. Now you want me to meet your family. And I can't. Because after a couple months, we'll get bored of each other."

"You mean *you'll* get bored." Kyle's forearm is flexed on the steering wheel.

"Yes, okay. I'll get bored. And I'll tell myself that it really doesn't matter anyway, because nothing does, and I'll hurt you. Just like I hurt everyone on that stupid list. And then we won't even be friends. Let's go back to being just friends now, while we still can."

"Ruby… I want to be more than your friend."

I squeeze my palms trying to calm this rising feeling of panic. "No, you don't."

He places a hand on my knee, and I look up into his chestnut eyes. "Yes, I do. I never told you before because I never thought I had a shot. And I didn't want to mess up our friendship. You talked about Harry and Sally, right? That's the thing… Sex didn't mess up their friendship. It was their feelings for each other. They were in love. If I didn't have any feelings for you, sure, everything could go back to normal. I could forget the feel of your lips and the taste of you. But, Ruby, I have feelings for you. Real feelings. I have for years."

"Years," I say, and it's not a question. As soon as we kissed, part of me knew. But I can't lose him in my life, and if we turn this into something more, I will.

"I know you don't do serious, but maybe—with us—it could be different."

I swallow back my tears. I can't lose my nerve. "Kyle, can we just go back to being friends? Please."

He moves his hand, our eyes locked on each other for a long moment, my heart in my throat. Kyle gets out of the car, grabbing my bags from the back. I get out, too, meeting him on the sidewalk. He hands me my bag. "I'll stay at my sister's tonight. I'll call you in the morning, and we can figure out when we want to head back."

"Kyle."

His jaw clenches. "Ruby, I can't go back to being only friends. I can't pretend that I don't love you, wholly and completely, with my entire being."

Tears threaten to fall, but I swallow them back. I will not cry. It won't help anything. I untie the flannel from my waist and hand it back to him, not sure what else to do or what else to say but wanting to give him something.

He shakes his head, placing his hand on mine. "Keep it. Put it in your breakup case."

And with that, he gets back in his truck and drives away.

CHAPTER 20

Check-in is the easiest thing I've done all day. I grab my key and head to the room as if I'm walking through a fog. Kyle loves me. Kyle's loved me for years. And I…fuck. I don't even know what I said. I blacked out. I don't even think I said anything. I just tried to give him back his shirt.

Curling up on the bed, shirt still in my hand, I inhale deeply. Woodsmoke and wool never smelled so good. What is wrong with me? There is no better man than Kyle. He's honest and loyal. He says what he means. And it's the most intense sex I've ever had in my entire life. So what is the problem?

I picture us together, really together. Him moving in. His soap in my bathroom. Moving things out of my grandmother's room to make space for his stuff. My stomach twists. No. We don't have a future together. It's best to stay the course. To find companions when needed but keep it light. It's fun until it's not. Then move on.

That's how it was with Nick and me. We were hot and heavy for nearly a year. But we still had our own space. Our own friends. Sure, we talked about moving in a couple of times, but we always decided it was best to keep our own space.

When we ended, there were no hard feelings on either side. There's no way this ring is from him, and I'm going to prove it.

AFTER CHANGING into a tight sweater and trying to run a brush through my hair, I read the notes from Heather.

Nick works in construction.

That hasn't changed. But there's literally nothing else.

I have his number. Maybe I should just text him. Or maybe this town is as small as Fortune Falls, and everybody knows everybody.

Heading down to the front desk, I approach the clerk, a young man with long brown hair and a thin nose, probably in his early twenties, if I had to guess. "Excuse me. Do you, by any chance, know Nick Mortimer?" I scroll through my phone and find a picture.

The young man tilts his head. "He looks kind of familiar. If he likes to party, half the town is doing SantaCon."

Nick definitely likes to party. "SantaCon?"

"Yeah. A bunch of people dress up like Santa, ride bikes, and hit up all the bars. They start a few towns over and end up here."

Picturing swerving bikes and icy roads, I say, "Sounds safe."

The kid chuckles. "It's a lot of fun. Last year, I lost my pants."

"Cool." I try not to scowl, because it doesn't actually sound cool at all. "Do you know when they end up around here?"

He nods. "Usually around ten or so."

Nope. That's too late.

"Where are they now?"

The kid pulls out his phone and taps the screen. "Hmm. It looks like thirteen minutes ago, they were at the Hungry Hippo."

"Where's that?"

"It's on the very edge of town. They might be closer to this area earlier than ten. I'm off in an hour. I could give you a ride." The kid smiles, slow and in a way I think he thinks is sexy.

My stomach twists. Nope. Not happening.

The kid must sense my hesitation, because he says, "Or we have a row of loaner bikes out front for guests."

"Perfect. Awesome. Thanks."

The kid gives me rough directions to the bar they last posted from, and I thank him again.

I head out into the cold, zipping up my cropped puffer and tugging on my red hat. Tightening the strap of my purse, I climb onto the bike. The air is cool on my cheeks but feels refreshing. It's about an eight-mile ride to the Hungry Hippo, according to my map. Easy peasy.

That is until I get to the massive hill that's between the bar and me. I stand to push the pedals down harder. My thighs are burning, and my head is flooding with flashes of Kyle's mouth on them. His hands gripping my ass. My heart pounds as I try to push through the thoughts and up this hill. What is going on with me? I've had sex before. Mind-blowing sex. What is it about Kyle that keeps my mind playing our time together over and over like a broken jukebox?

Halfway up the hill, my legs shaking, sweat dripping down my back despite the arctic temperatures, I hop off the bike and push it the rest of the way. This area is cute, too. The streets are lined with brick buildings. The Hungry Hippo is easy to find, mostly because of the group of about twelve Santas, both men and women, standing in front of it smoking, drinking, and generally wobbling on their feet. One of the more petite female Santas in a red dress with white fur trim catches the curb wrong, and I drop the bike, rushing to catch her by the elbow before she sprains an ankle.

"Whoa. Watch it, girl," she slurs as she stumbles away, blowing out a plume of smoke.

"You're welcome," I call out. God, it feels like being at work during the sandcastle festival. Too many people, too many drinks, not enough water.

Picking up the bike, I lean it against the side of the building and head inside. My feet sink into a bouncy mix of sawdust and peanut shells on the floor. It's not entirely unpleasant, but how do they ever clean it? Do they get new sawdust periodically? Spray bleach?

The bar is a sea of red. Santa suits fill the space. But not only Santas. There's a man dressed as a Christmas tree. There are quite a few men in festive suits, most of them without shirts underneath their jackets. There are even some women in elegant dresses—one in an amazing black velvet number with a full skirt. Very Grace Kelly in *Rear Window*. One tall man is dressed as Buddy the Elf. I scan the faces, searching for Nick, as the speakers blast "Rocking Around the Christmas Tree."

Heading to the bar, I order a whiskey. The bartender gives me a hefty pour. After I thank him, I turn, leaning my back against the bar and scanning the crowd. I find him at the pool table, leaning over, lining up a shot. His sandy blond hair is moving into his eyes, and he brushes it out of the way. He takes his long, white, obviously fake beard and pulls it down so it's hanging around his neck. He's wearing bright-red Santa pants with black suspenders and no shirt. His muscles are still as defined as I remember.

He makes the shot, sinking a solid with ease. The next he misses by a hair. I turn back to the bar. This is stupid. What am I even doing here? What if the ring really is from him? What then?

Then I'll know. And I'll give it back. If it is from him, it was probably a wild, harebrained idea he had one day that flitted away like so many others before it.

I can do this.

I down the rest of my whiskey and head over to the pool table. The game looks over. Nick and the other man are clasping hands. Someone changes the jukebox, and the music shifts to "All I Want for Christmas is You."

Nick leans the pool stick against the wall. He grabs his beer as I step up to the high-top table. Nick's eyebrows rise as he keeps drinking his beer, one large gulp after the next. I wait.

He slams the empty can down on the table and wipes his mouth. "Holy fucking shit. Ruby!"

I smile. He picks me up and swings me around, my leg hitting something—or more like someone—along the way. "Nick, put me down."

He does, but his hands linger on my hips for a beat longer than necessary. "Come on. Let's get a drink."

He grabs my hand, pulling me to the bar and ordering two Rainers before I can say that it seems like he's already had three too many. The bartender hands us two sweating cans, and Nick slams his into mine, sending foam shooting out of the top. He sips his, and we find seats at some open bar stools.

"Ruby fucking McVeigh."

"Nick fucking Mortimer."

He smiles, his blue eyes looking me up and down. "You look good."

I sigh, because this is absolutely not what I'm here for.

Nick places a hand on my leg, and I can feel eyes on us. Scanning the crowd, through a sea of people dancing to Mariah Carey, I find Mrs. Claus in a very short skirt eyeing us from across the bar.

I move my legs, motioning with my head toward Mrs. Claus. "I don't think she likes that."

He picks up his beer, shrugging. "We're not that serious. She's just a friend."

I nod slowly and wonder if that's how he described me. Unzipping my purse, I pull out the ring from the inside pocket. Nick doesn't register it, placing his hand back on my knee. I hold it up to his eye level.

"Are you proposing, Rubes?"

I search his face for any recognition, any hint of a smile that might mean he's messing with me. But there's nothing there.

"I'm not. Were you going to?"

"The fuck?" He shakes his head.

I explain about finding the ring and the little note. I don't explain about the breakup suitcase, and instead say it was in a box of stuff from him.

He takes the ring from my hand, peering closely at it, turning it in the light, the gem sparkling. Then he hands it back to me.

"Never seen it before. We had fun." He moves his hand up to my thigh. "A lot of fun. But you and I—we're not the marrying kind. We're too smart for that." He moves his hand an inch higher. "It's all chemicals flying around. We're animals stuck on a rock spinning in space. Might as well have fun."

It's a familiar diatribe, one I've given so many times. If you don't get too serious, no one gets hurt. But today, right now, the words feel hollow. And the fact that I can see what he's saying is bullshit spikes my heart rate, makes sweat break out on the back of my neck.

He moves his hand a little higher. "Speaking of fun... Wanna dance?"

"Yes." I stand and walk out toward the sea of people, Nick right behind me, his hand on the waistband of my jeans.

"Snowman" by Sia pulses, and we move to the beat. Nick is making a ridiculous face as he grabs for my waist. I turn around, backing up into him so I don't have to see him. Moving. Trying to dance this rising panic away like Kevin Bacon in *Footloose*. But it just gets stronger. The song ends, and I practically run off the dance floor down a hallway marked restroom. The door is locked. I wait. Sweat coats my back, so I take off my sweater and wait by the wall in my white tank top.

Nick comes around the corner. "There you are."

He pushes me into the wall, running his hand up my body, grazing my breast, to my neck. His other hand fiddles with my waistband. Making quick moves, he unbuttons my jeans. And it's all happening so fast, my mind is reeling, trying to figure out how to stop this or if I should.

He brings his mouth to where my jaw meets my ear and whispers as he unzips my jeans, "I want you."

Honestly, if this had happened a week ago, I would have been all about it. I'd have dragged him into the bathroom, and we'd have made out like there was no tomorrow.

But there is a tomorrow. And for once, I want to act like there is.

"Nick," I say as the bathroom door opens.

Nick wheels around, blocking my body with his like I'm naked behind him.

The person from the restroom walks past us, holding a hand up to shield their eyes, then drops it as his eyes find mine.

Kyle's face goes white as a sheet. "Ruby?"

"Oh, dude!" Nick moves a hand to clasp Kyle's but keeps standing in front of me. "It's good to see you."

Kyle looks at Nick's offered hand and back at me. His eyes search mine, and when I don't say anything, he strides away. I come out from behind Nick and go after him.

"Kyle, wait."

I catch him by the bar, asking the bartender for his tab.

I touch his arm, but he pulls it away. "It's not what it looked like."

His eyes move up and down me, landing on my face with a frown. "Your pants are undone."

I close my eyes. Because shit. This looks bad. I zip and button them as Kyle signs his credit slip. "Kyle, it's really not—"

He holds up a hand. "Ruby, it's fine. You never made me any promises. In fact, you did exactly what you said you would. Look, I'm going to stay at my Chloe's for an extra day. She's going to ride back with me to spend Christmas at my dad's in Fortune. You should get the train back."

Kyle heads toward a petite woman standing by the dart board with dark hair pulled back in a ponytail. She looks so much like Kyle that she has to be his sister.

I grab Kyle's arm, and he turns around. There's no anger in his eyes, just a deep sorrow, and my stomach plummets. "Kyle, nothing happened."

"You know why I'm not friends with Nick? He talked about you like you meant nothing. And when I confronted him about it, he tried to turn it around that I was jealous."

"Kyle…" I try to reach for him again, but he backs away.

"He was right. I was jealous. I *am* jealous. He didn't deserve you then, and he doesn't deserve you now." He turns. "Have fun, Ruby."

I watch, frozen to the spot, as Kyle and his sister walk out the door.

CHAPTER 21

S hit. I take a seat at the bar, ordering another whiskey.

Nick comes and finds me, taking the seat next to me. "I see Kyle is pleasant as always."

It's such a ridiculous statement, because Kyle *is* pleasant. Kyle is wonderful. Kyle just doesn't like Nick and never has. And now I know why.

Nick places his hand on my thigh, his pecs flexing as he does. Across the bar, the woman who's been shooting daggers at us all night walks out the door.

"Your girlfriend left," I say, but he doesn't look. His eyes are fixed on me.

"There's plenty of Mrs. Clauses in the sea." He squeezes my thigh.

I pick up his hand and move it off my leg, plopping it into his lap. "How long have you two been dating?"

He doesn't answer, just sips his beer.

"How long were *we* dating?"

"Were we dating, Ruby? I seem to remember you saying several times we were only having fun."

He's not wrong. But how much of that was me protecting myself against this? Him flirting with another girl. Or, what's even worse, what if he didn't? What if we worked out and were mad for each other, then lost each other to cancer or a car accident? What if unforeseen circumstances ripped us apart, like it did my grandparents? Like it took my grandmother from me?

But seeing Nick here, doing the same casual, none-of-it-matters thing with another girl turns my stomach. He's a honeybee, flitting from flower to flower, never stopping long enough to really drink someone in. I can see it so clearly, because it's me.

I find my coat still hanging on the hook underneath the bar and shrug it back on. "Goodbye, Nick."

He calls after me in that pouting tone that used to do something for me but now does less than nothing.

This superficial bullshit is not what I want from my life. This isn't fun. Not anymore.

Shouldering my way through Santa after Santa, I walk out the door. I grab the bike, turn on the light, and ride down the street, the cool air whipping my hair back.

Once I'm back at the hotel, I try calling Kyle, but it goes straight to voicemail. I try three more times before I fall into a fitful sleep. In the morning, I pack up my stuff, buy a train ticket online, and check out, all the while texting and calling Kyle with absolutely no response.

On the train, I put my phone away. It's going to take more than a phone call to prove to Kyle I'm not the same person I was at the start of this trip. That he can trust me.

I sigh, leaning against the window and watching the mountains roll by. *Can* he trust me? I've been so wrong about all of it. I'd been sure I hadn't hurt any of the guys who the ring could've been from—I'd been wrong. The only one I actually hadn't hurt was Nick, and if I'm being completely honest with myself, it's because he hurt me.

Kyle asked me why I kept the breakup case in the first place if none of the relationships were serious, if none of them mattered. I didn't have a good answer at the time. But now I see... I wanted them to mean something, and if I had let them, they would've.

It's dark by the time I get home, and my house is freezing. I dump all my things by the door, kick off my boots, and start a fire. I click on the television and catch the end of *Scrooged*. Kyle and I missed this part at the motel. My cheeks warm at the memory of his mouth on my…everything.

Bill Murray is inspiring the crowd to take a chance, that the miracle can happen to you. He's ready for *the miracle*.

And tears form in the corner of my eye. It's silly. It's not even that great of a speech, but something about it strikes me. I *am* ready for it. I'm ready to step into my life instead of fearing it might end at any moment, not getting close to people because they might be ripped away from me. I head to my bedroom, but my eye catches instead on my grandma's room. I flick on the light.

It's the same as it was five years ago when she passed. Her comforter. Her clothes in the closet. Her sewing table in the corner. I see now how utterly sad this would make her. She wouldn't want it like this, frozen in time.

"Grandma, I hope you don't mind, but it's time. Time for me to start living my life like the choices I make matter. Like my life matters. And the first step is a room upgrade." I roll up my sleeves. "I'm moving in."

I CARRY the sewing machine to the garage but leave the little desk by the window, setting my laptop on it. I order a new comforter online. My grandma's will work for now, but I want to truly transform the space. Next, I tackle the closet, boxing up clothes to donate to the local shelter and picking out a few sweaters that are cute on me. I take boxes down, opening them to see what's inside and then moving them to the garage.

Finally, I take out the last box, tucked away on the ground in the very back. It's not an old cardboard box like most of them have been. No, this one is more like a small trunk. It's wooden and heavy. I bring it out to the living room and make myself a cup of tea, setting it by the couch. The hinges squeak as I open the chest.

Inside are dozens of photos. I pick one at random and find my grandmother and grandfather posing in front of this very house, hands clasped together. The next is one of my grandmother holding either my mom or my uncle as a scrunchy-faced baby, my grandfather practically beaming behind her.

Flashes of my own memories of my grandparents in this house come to mind as I flip through the photos. Them dancing in the kitchen while bread baked in the oven. Easter egg hunts where they held hands in matching lawn chairs and cheered me on. They were so happy.

Sure, when Grandma lost him, she was devastated. I was little, but I remember Grandma would cry sometimes, or she'd get this far-off look in her eye. And later when I lost her… I swallow hard, running my fingers over the edges of the photos and pulling another one out.

It never occurred to me before how much worse it would've been to never have had those moments at all. What if Grandma tried to spare herself the heartbreak of losing Grandpa and missed out on a lifetime of love?

If I never give anyone a chance. If I never let anyone in. If I continue to flit from flower to flower, I'll spare myself some pain— maybe. But I'll definitely lose out on so much joy. Possibly a lifetime worth.

I don't want to be a honeybee anymore. I want to be an eagle. I want to build something. And there's only one person I want to build it with.

But I may have really, truly fucked that up.

THE LIGHT IS a soft golden yellow as it streams through the gauzy curtains in my grandma's—no, strike that, my room. It's Christmas Eve, and there's still a lot of work to do. Throwing on Kyle's flannel and some sweats, I head to the kitchen. I make myself a cup of coffee, tie my hair back, and start moving things from my room to…my new room.

Clothes in the closet, books on the shelf, and most of the day later, there are just a few things left to move. My heart leaps into my throat as my phone vibrates on the nightstand.

I answer it without looking. "Kyle."

"No, sweetie. It's Mom."

As nice as it is to hear from her, my heart sinks back down to my chest with a heavy thud. "Hey."

"Woof. Don't sound so happy to hear from me. Should I have taken some time off and been there? You know the holiday season is so busy here. I offered to get you a ticket on the ship. In fact, I still can. Want to come on the Valentine's cruise to the Virgin Islands?"

"No, Mom. It's fine. It's not that."

"What's going on? Because you sound like your dog died. Oh my God, did you get a dog?"

"No." But maybe I should. I've always wanted a dog, and I've never gotten one because it's such a huge commitment. But now I'm ready for big commitments.

"What is it, then, sweetie?"

I plop down on the couch and let it all out. About the ring, about the love-life list, and the PG version of what happened with Kyle and me.

At which point, my mom whoops. "Finally."

"Finally?"

"Yes. I've known you were in love with Kyle for years. I was hoping you would realize it someday. The way you talk about him. Even in high school, you were two peas in a pod. Always there for each other."

I laugh, because I'm shocked that, once again, I'm the last one to see it. "I messed it all up, though. Kyle… I don't know if he'll ever talk to me again. And I still haven't found out who the ring is from."

"Who cares?"

"What?" This shocks me since my mom is mystery obsessed.

"Honey, that ring doesn't hold your future. Whoever that ring is from, it's the past. You need to focus on Kyle. He's your future."

I feel it in my bones that she's right, but it's too late. I fucked it up.

My mom says, "What you need to do is get a giant boombox. I think there's one in the garage…"

I laugh. "No, Mom."

"You have to show him how you feel."

"I don't know. You should've seen his face. I can't. I'm going to give him some space."

"Ruby Tuesday, space isn't always the answer. Sometimes the answer is taking a chance, putting yourself out there, and showing you care."

"I'll think about it, Mom. Thanks for calling."

"Merry Christmas Eve, honey."

ROLLING UP MY SLEEVES, I get back to work. I pull the breakup case out from under the bed, open it, and begin looking through it. I box some of it up to donate. Most of it is junk, though. I keep some photos. While it's time to let go of my past relationships and who I was in them, some of the memories and mementos will stay. Because despite all my protesting, they were real relationships, with real emotions. But storing all my feelings about them in a suitcase isn't helping anyone. Once it's emptied, I tip it over to get some of the dust out, and an envelope slips out of the side pocket, *Ruby* scrawled shakily across the front.

My heart catches in my throat as I stare at the handwriting—my grandmother's handwriting.

I open the envelope with trembling fingers and pull out the letter inside, taking a seat on the bed as I do.

My Dearest Ruby,

I wasn't quite sure where to stash this letter. It needs to be somewhere you will find it when you're ready and not when it might feel like unwelcome advice. Or, heaven forbid, one of my famous lectures.

I laugh. Grandma really could lecture with the best of them. Grandpa always joked they rivaled any sermon from Pastor Mark.

You know I have a knack for inserting myself where I'm not necessarily wanted, so the breakup case it is. Yes, I know you have been using my mother's old suitcase as a shrine to all the boys you've dumped. I see you. I see you hiding away, not letting anyone in. And I know it's all my fault. It was hard on all of us when we lost your grandfather, then there was my first cancer diagnosis. As brave as you've been over the years, I know you've been terrified. And you built walls. Not from me, but from others.

Part of me thought, good for her. Protecting herself. This way she won't get hurt. But I see now I should've said something sooner. Sweets, you have to open your heart to the possibilities of life.

I went through a period in my late teens when I lost someone close to me. I was so in love with him. His name was Shawn. And he was lovely. He asked me to marry him. The ring is in the pocket, too, if you haven't already found it. I said yes. He was wild. Full of life. But one night, he was in a terrible accident. He didn't make it.

I met your grandfather two years later. When I first met him, he asked me out to the movies. I said no. I didn't want to hurt like that again, ever. But he kept asking. And there was something about him. He kept showing up. Lending a helping hand when needed. I knew I could count on him.

I said yes. And the rest is history.

Ruby, my sweet, sensitive girl. And yes, you are sensitive. That's why you've built these walls. You have to at least build a door. You have to let life in. I'm not even talking about love. If you want to be single, that's fine. But you have to live.

And call your mom. She loves you. She's always just been so busy. Never could sit still, that girl.

I love you to the moon and back, my shiny Ruby. If you're not ready to hear all this now, put it away and read it every two years. I know one day you will be.

Love, Grandma

Grandma always had impeccable timing. I wonder when she put this in here, and my heart aches with how much I'd like to ask her. To tell her that she's right. God, she'd love that.

I say it aloud anyway. "You're right. I hear you. I'm going to build a door—no, better yet, a nest."

CHAPTER 22

After dusting off my bike in the garage, pumping the tires, and making sure the light on the front still works, I head out. The sun set hours ago, and the night sky is filled with stars. The snow has all melted off the roads, but the air has that smell that it'll snow again sooner rather than later. The houses are all lit up, the Christmas lights twinkling, the chimneys smoking, the windows glowing a soft amber.

I ride to Kyle's house. The Christmas tree sparkles in the front window. His truck isn't in the driveway, though. Then I remember he said he was taking his sister to his dad's house. Of course, he's at his dad's. It's freaking Christmas Eve.

Maybe I should wait until tomorrow. I can talk to him one on one. He might not want me to ambush him in front of his family. But the thought of going home alone, without at least telling him how I feel… I can't stomach it.

After a nearly twenty-minute ride, I arrive at a red house with a white picket fence around it. I lean my bike against the fence and swap my bike helmet for the soft red hat Kyle bought me in Beachside. Unzipping my coat, I set it on the bike, relishing the cool air after the ride warmed me up.

In the yard is a huge tree, a tire swing swaying in the breeze. The front window is lit by a Christmas tree. The porch light is on. On the porch swing, a beer on the table next to him and knitting needles in his hands, is Kyle.

I smooth down my—his—shirt and try to do the same with my hair, but there's no point. The wind has styled my curls into a wild thing, and I hope that he likes it.

Kyle rises from the swing, coming to the railing. "Ruby?"

"Hey," I say, and he comes down to meet me on the stone path.

He looks me up and down, smiling. "Nice hat."

"Somebody once told me I look good in red."

He smiles, that dimple popping.

"I found out who the ring was from…"

The smile is gone. "Nick. Right—"

"No." I grab his hand. "Not Nick. Seeing Nick was a disaster. Nothing happened. In the hallway, I mean. I know it looked…bad. But really, nothing happened."

He searches my face, but he doesn't say anything. He's still holding my hand, so that's a good sign.

I continue. "Seeing Nick kind of woke me up a bit."

"How so?"

I smile. "He's a honeybee, and I used to be, too. But I don't want to be that anymore."

Kyle's brow furrows. "You're a honeybee?"

I sigh. "I'm messing this up. My mom suggested I bring a boombox, and I should've listened."

He raises his eyebrows. "You talked about me with your mom?"

"I did. I told her I have feelings for you, and you know what? She wasn't surprised. Maybe she was right about doing something a little flashier, but I thought what you would like the most would be if I came with no tricks. No props. Just me and the truth."

He squeezes my hand but doesn't pull me close. "And what is that? What's the truth?"

I grab his other hand and look up into his eyes, almost black in the dark night. "I love you. Not as a friend—although I love you as a friend, too. I want to sleep with you."

"Whoa, forward."

I laugh. "No. Although I want to do that, too. But I mean really sleep, in your arms. Or next to you, because we can't always sleep snuggled up, and I always want to go to bed with you. And to wake up with you. I want to plan a future with you. We can figure out what you want to do about the bar. And what I'm going to do with my baking. I want to get a dog."

"A dog?"

"Yes. I want us to pick him out together. I want to build a nest."

"I'm pretty sure dogs like beds."

I smile and shake my head. "With you. Like the eagles."

He nods, a soft smile on his face and a tear in the corner of his eye. "You aren't worried about getting bored? I can be pretty boring."

"Everyone is boring. I'm into boring." His mouth falls open, and I gently bring my hand to his chin, shutting it. "I'm kidding. But sometimes life is boring. I want to be with you for all the exciting stuff, sure, but all the doing-laundry-on-a-Sunday-afternoon stuff, too. I want to live my life with you."

"For how long?" There are worry lines around his mouth.

I step closer, wrapping my arms around his neck. "As long as you'll have me."

He leans down, whispering, "I'll have you."

Our lips meet. His are soft and taste like the bitterness of the beer he was drinking, but also a little sweet. We kiss in the cool night, Christmas lights shimmering around us and stars shining brightly above us. Kyle picks me up and swings me around, and I laugh.

"Want to come in?" he asks as he puts me down. "It's a full house, so I'm sleeping in the basement on the pullout. My older sister is here with her kids from Seattle, and Chloe is in the other bedroom. Everyone's already in bed, so we'll have to be quiet."

I smile. "I can be quiet."

He frowns, lowering one eyebrow.

I swat at him. "I can."

"Remains to be seen."

"Well, if you could keep your hands to yourself…"

He pulls me in close again, bringing his lips to the shell of my ear.

"Not going to happen. Ever." Moving his hand down, he gives my ass a swift swat, sending a warm tingle through my body. "Now get in there."

"Yes, sir," I say, stepping as quietly as I can into the house.

I WAKE up snuggled next to Kyle on the pullout sofa in his dad's basement. Kyle's hand is resting lightly on my stomach under my shirt. I move the slightest bit, and he stirs, moving his hand up and grazing the underside of my breast.

Backing my ass into him, I can feel he's excited. He pulls my bra down, releasing my breast and squeezing it in his hand.

There's a thundering of feet above us and the squeals of children. "Santa came."

Kyle groans. "What I wouldn't give for a lockable door right about now."

I turn over and face him, tucking my breast back into my bra. I give him a soft kiss. "We better get up there. Santa came."

"Mmmm. I'd like to come," he grumbles.

I laugh, and he nuzzles into my neck. "Come on. I want to meet your family."

He snaps back, the smile on his face bigger than I've ever seen it. "Will you say that again?"

I slowly say each word. "I want to meet your family."

Kyle hops out of bed, stepping into his discarded jeans. "Hot damn. Let's go."

We head upstairs, and Kyle's dad gives me a huge smile. "Ruby, it's so nice to see you."

I smile back. "Thanks for letting me crash—"

He squeezes my shoulder as he walks past, delivering a cup of coffee to Chloe. "Not crashing. You're always welcome."

Kyle introduces me to his sisters, Maria the eldest and Chloe the one from the bar. Chloe scoots over on the couch, patting the spot next to her as Kyle goes to grab coffee from the kitchen.

"So," Chloe says. "You and Kyle." She lifts and lowers her eyebrows.

I laugh. "Uh..."

She leans in, lowering her voice. "You two... Look, he's loved you a long, long time. Don't fuck this up."

Her brown eyes level me with such sincerity, my heart squeezes. I don't want to fuck this up.

I place my hand on hers. "I won't. I promise."

Kyle brings me a cup of coffee, smiling. "What are you two up to?"

I take the cup as Chloe smiles sweetly.

"Girl talk." She winks at me and gets up from the loveseat. "You can have my spot."

Kyle sits close to me, his arm draped over my shoulder, as his nieces open their Christmas presents.

There's one last present under the tree, and Kyle grabs it, handing it to me. "Merry Christmas."

It's wrapped in green paper with a red ribbon wrapped around it several times. Kyle sits next to me and whispers in my ear, "Save the ribbon for later."

My cheeks flood with heat, and I swat him, hissing in his ear, "Not in front of *the fam*."

He laughs. "Open it."

I unwind the excessive amount of ribbon then tear into the paper. Inside, my fingers find soft wool. I pull out a long, red scarf. There are a few holes here and there, and the lines are uneven in places. The smile that overtakes my face is so wide, it hurts. "It's perfect. When did you make this?"

He snuggles into my side. "I've been working on it. I tried to match the hat."

I wrap the scarf around my neck. "Thank you."

His dad makes pancakes for everyone. We sit in front of the tree, wrapping paper scattered on the floor, a fire in the hearth, and Kyle's hand on my thigh. Everyone is chatting and stuffing their faces. It's warm, cozy, and perfect.

We spend most of the day there, stealing kisses, Kyle's hand always somewhere on my body. The small of my back. My hand. My thigh. In the afternoon, he leans in to whisper in my ear, "Let's get out of here."

We say goodbye to everyone and head for the truck. Kyle throws my bike in the back and starts the engine. His hand finds my thigh as we drive down the road. All the touching, seeing how sweet he is with his family… It's been all-day foreplay, and I've had enough.

Shrugging off my coat, I undo my bra and take it off underneath the shirt. Then I unbutton my flannel…one slow button at a time.

Kyle glances over at me. "Are you too hot?"

I open the shirt. The cool air in the truck hits my bare skin, and my nipples grow hard. Kyle's pupils double in size.

"You tell me." I lift my breasts, squeezing them in my hands.

"Oh, fuck," he grits out. He cranks the wheel to pull over.

"Drive to my place." I unbutton my jeans and unzip them, the sound slicing through the small space. "Fast."

Kyle grips the wheel so tightly, I worry he might break it as I kick off my boots and shimmy out of my pants.

"Your house is too far," Kyle says as he turns down a dirt road.

"It's like ten minutes away."

"Like I said, too far." He puts his hand back on my thigh, running it up higher and higher until he finds my silky underwear, and he groans.

The dirt road leads to a gravel parking area with an entrance to the beach. The waves are rolling in hard and fast, like there might be a storm coming. He pulls the truck into a tucked-away spot by the trees.

He moves his hand away, turns off the engine, and shifts in his seat to face me. "Lay your seat back."

I do as I'm told, moving the seat all the way back and laying it down as far as it'll go.

"Take off the flannel and throw it into the back."

I take it off, tossing it over my shoulder.

"Now touch yourself. Show me what you like."

I move my hands over my breasts, down to my underwear, sliding them off and throwing them into the back as well. I swirl my finger through my slit under Kyle's heavy gaze, his eyes hooded and hungry. Slipping one finger inside, I cry out. Kyle gets out of the truck, walking around the front in determined strides. He opens my door, and the cold air hits me. He slides back into the truck, lifting me up and putting me on his lap. The bulge in his pants is hard underneath me. I turn to face him.

We lock eyes.

"Hey," I whisper.

"Hey yourself."

I unzip his pants, and as I release him from the confines of the denim, he lets out a heavy sigh. His face is lit by the waning sun, his strong hands are planted on my hips, and his gorgeous cock is between my legs, waiting for me. He's beautiful.

"Do you have a condom?"

He moves a little, reaching into his back pocket and pulling one out.

I tear it open, unrolling it slowly on him as his eyelids flutter.

"Are you ready for me?" he asks.

And I smile. "I wasn't. But I am now."

It's the truth, and I don't mean the sex. I mean him. I mean this feeling I get when I'm near him. When I'm wrapped in his arms. When we were spending time with his family. He feels like home.

I lift myself and lower onto him, my breasts grazing his soft shirt. Going slowly, I lower all the way down as he watches. I moan as he goes deeper than he ever has before, deeper than anyone ever has before.

"Oh, fuck, Ruby."

I moan as I lift and lower, consuming him the whole way every time. He moves his hands to my ass and grips me, keeping me in place but letting me set the pace.

The pressure starts to build, and I move faster, trying to fill this need for him. Over and over, faster and faster. I call out his name as he squeezes my ass. I clench. Everything clenches. And I can feel him release as I'm tight around him.

I fall onto his chest, his shirt soft on my cheek. He runs a hand down my hair and along my back, leaving goosebumps in its wake.

I look up into his face, and his eyes find mine. "I love you."

His dimple pops. "I love you."

We sit there—listening to the waves roll in and out, my cheek on his chest, Kyle's steady heartbeat under my ear—for a long time. There's no hurry. We have all the time in the world. All the time the universe allows. And I'm done being afraid of how long or short that may be.

ONE YEAR LATER

Cinnamon, sugar, gingerbread, and a light hint of impending snow fill the air. The Saturday market is packed, and with one hour left to go, my treats are almost sold out. My booth, Whisk Taker, sells cinnamon rolls, gingerbread cookies, eclairs, beignets—a fan favorite and always the first to sell out—and whatever seasonal thing my heart desires. I've even been hired to bake a wedding cake in the new year. It's not my own bakery—yet—but it's going really well.

I love the market. I love my little business. Today, however, I'm counting the minutes until Kyle comes to help me break it down. My feet are swollen, and I have heartburn. It seems like as soon as my morning sickness subsided, heartburn took over. At twenty-six weeks, my belly is huge. I'm not sure how I'm supposed to walk around and function if it gets much bigger.

Over the last year, Kyle and I have made a lot of plans. He's made some awesome improvements to The Vern. He added locally baked goods to the brunch menu, courtesy of me. He hired a manager, too, so he's able to do his real estate a few days a week. During the summer, he moved into my place, coincidently, around the same time we found out about our little surprise.

My eye catches Heather's through the aisle of booths. I wave to her and hand my customer their change. As she gets closer, I see that her face is puffy, her eyes red. My stomach swoops uncomfortably, and I place a hand on my round belly.

"Heather, what's going on?"

She sniffles. "He fucking did it again."

My heart joins my stomach. I'm not going to lie… As much as I have tried to like Theo, I don't. I don't trust the guy, and with good reason, it seems.

"Oh, honey."

She walks behind the counter and into my waiting arms.

"It was the same woman. They never ended things."

Heather plops down onto a crate, and I take the open seat. "I'm so sorry. Come over. You can stay the night. We can make Margs and Meg night early this week." The margs have been peppermint tea for me, but we've kept up the tradition.

"No. I can't tonight." She wipes a tear and looks away quickly.

"Why not?" I ask, narrowing my eyes. Heather never turns down a margarita.

She takes a large inhale. "You're busy."

"No, I'm not. Kyle's going to pick me up soon. Literally my plan is to lie on my couch. Come lie on my couch with me."

"Right. I meant I'm busy." She stands. "I should go. My friend Aubrey is having a rough time, too. We're going to FaceTime."

I stand, taking a bit longer than Heather to do so, and we hug. She buries her face in my hair.

"I love you. If you change your mind, come over."

She nods, the motion moving my hair. "I will."

Whisk Taker sells out thirty minutes before the market closes, so I text Kyle to come get me. He drives the truck up as close as he can. Roscoe bounds out of the truck, running right over to me and wagging his tail.

I scratch behind his ears. I got Roscoe a few weeks before Kyle moved in. A family down the street was moving and couldn't take him with them. He's the sweetest golden retriever and already housebroken.

Roscoe follows me as I start to lift the pastry cabinet onto the cart.

Kyle shoos me away. "I got it. Go sit in the car. You look beat."

I fluff my hair, throw my scarf over my shoulder, and adjust my red beanie. "Well, hello to you, too."

He smiles, that adorable dimple popping. Striding over in two long steps, he wraps his arms around me and brings his lips to mine. When we part, he says, "You look beautiful as always."

I smile and lean into him, inhaling deeply. He rubs circles on my lower back, and I groan. "Ooh, yeah. Right there."

Roscoe wags his tail into our legs.

Kyle rubs a little harder, and a soft moan escapes my lips. He steps back. "We better cool it if we don't want to get kicked out of the market for public indecency."

Laughing, I pack a few things into the truck, and then, taking Kyle up on his offer, I go sit in the passenger seat, sinking into the soft leather. Roscoe joins me, climbing into the back.

Once everything is all packed up, Kyle gets in with a giant smile on his face. He looks at me, and there's something almost mischievous about it.

"What?" I ask.

"Are you okay with a slight detour?"

Hmmm. My feet are screaming no. But my heart, looking at his excited face, overrules them. "Always."

We drive down the familiar streets of Fortune Falls, past The Vern, past the bookstore. "Are we headed to your dad's?"

He smiles, his dimple popping. It's his *I-have-a-secret* smile. "Nope."

I know this is the way. But if we're not headed there… "Where are we going?"

He smirks. "You'll see."

It's when he turns down the dirt road that I figure it out. He parks the truck tucked away under the trees near the narrow path to the beach, the ocean waves crashing beyond.

I smile, remembering our afternoon here, steaming up the windows. When we exchanged our first real "I love yous."

Kyle turns off the engine and turns to face me.

I put both hands on my belly. "I love your eternal optimism, but I really don't think we're both going to fit. Definitely not with enough room to fool around. And it might freak Roscoe out."

Kyle chuckles, and the sound is more delicious than anything I could ever bake.

I move the seat back. "I'm game to try."

He laughs more and gets out of the truck. He opens my door, offering me his hand. "Will you take a walk with me? A short one, I promise."

At the word "walk," Roscoe hops out of the truck, his tongue hanging out as he skips around Kyle.

I slip my hand into his. We stroll down the path, stepping over some roots and weaving around some overgrown bushes. This is definitely a secret entrance to the beach, and when we step onto the sand, it's well worth the extra effort. The beach stretches out for miles on one side and ends at a rock face on the other, with a cave and a thin waterfall trickling down.

The air is fresh and salty. It smells so good, I could gulp it down. We walk hand in hand toward the cave as a light snow falls. Roscoe bounds ahead, living his best dog life. A seal barks somewhere in the distance. I stop to look out at the waves, trying to spot it. And next to me, Kyle kneels in the sand, taking my hand in both of his.

I swear my heart stops. "Kyle, what are you doing?"

"Ruby, I love you. I've loved you for years. I love your adventurous spirit. I love your wild hair and your relentless attempts to tame it. I love how you love your friends. I love how you love me, with your whole body. I'm so impressed by your bravery this past year. And I was wondering if…"

He pulls a box out of his jacket pocket and opens it with a snap to reveal a gorgeous ring with a single diamond on a gold band sealed with vines. It's unique and absolutely stunning.

"Will you marry me?"

My heart races in my chest. I think of my grandma accepting that ring from the man she loved, only to have him cruelly ripped away from her. I've come a long way in overcoming my fear of commitment, but this feels like a lot.

I rub my belly. "You don't have to… I mean, just because of the baby…"

He stands, cupping my face in one hand and rubbing his thumb where my jaw meets my ear. "Ruby, even if there was no baby, I would want to be with you for the rest of my life. If you don't want to get married, that's cool." He closes the box shut and throws the ring box over his shoulder.

I gasp. "Kyle!"

Roscoe runs after it.

Kyle moves his hands down my body, smiling. "None of that matters. I want you and me. Forever."

"Forever." I smile. That's what I want, too. If we're going to do it, we might as well have a party to celebrate. "Yes."

"Yes?"

Roscoe nuzzles into my leg.

"Yes, Kyle Papadopoulos. I will marry you."

"She said yes!" He picks me up and swings me around, plants a soft, warm kiss on my lips, and then sets me down, looking around the sand behind him. "Shit."

Roscoe nuzzles into my hand, whimpering. I look and see he'd retrieved the ring box.

I take it from his mouth and wipe off the sand and slobber. "Did you train him to do that?"

Kyle laughs, grabbing the box. He opens it, takes the ring out, and slips it onto my finger.

I throw my arms around his neck, watching the ring twinkle in the gray winter light. "Did Heather know about this?"

He smiles, bringing his lips to my neck. "I wanted to be sure I was picking the right ring."

I smile as shivers move down my spine at his kisses. "Let's go see if there's enough room in the truck."

He backs up, his eyes wide, and I lift and lower my eyebrows.

"You don't have to ask me twice."

We race back to the truck, Roscoe running behind us, my blood pumping through my veins and warming my cheeks. Once we're at the truck, Roscoe hops into the bed, and Kyle leans me against it. His lips meet mine, and just like every time since that first kiss in the carriage, my heart beats wildly in my chest. He kisses me. The snow falls lightly around us, the ocean waves roll in the distance, the ring is snug on my slightly swollen finger, and our future stretches before us. The good and the bad, the ups and the down. The unknown. All of it uncertain except our love. And for once, I'm not scared of it.

The End

ACKNOWLEDGMENTS

Thank you for being here for another Fortune Falls story. There will be more coming out next year. And thank you to all the readers (and cps, I'm looking at you Francie) that demanded justice for Kyle. This story was the most fun to write.

Thank you again to my sister Alaina for EVERYTHING.

Thank you to my romance girlies, Robin Blackburn and Stephanie Paul. You helped me shape this into something that I think turned out pretty special. I value our work together and our friendship so much.

Thank you to my parents for all your love and support and especially to my mom who told me over and over that I could do anything, and I believed it.

Thank you to my daughter and my husband. You two are my world.

Thank you Jenny Rarden for helping me make sense. Your copy edits are amazing.

Thank you Andrea Halland for your impeccable proofread and little heart comments that keep me going.

And a huge thank you to all the readers of this book, The Now in Forever and The Art of the Meet Cute Thank you for spending your time with me and the characters so dear to my heart. I hope you'll consider doing it again.

ABOUT THE AUTHOR

I received a BFA in mixed media studio art. With a degree in the arts and no solid plan, I've had the opportunity to hold many different jobs; video store manager, barista, photographer's assistant, toy store clerk, and yoga instructor at a retreat in Puerto Rico are just a few. Hands on research for her books.

Currently, when I'm not writing, you can find me working at a title one elementary school library, crafting with her little girl, or hosting the podcast, *So I Wrote a Book...Now What*, where I interview fellow authors about their revision process.

Want to join my newsletter?

ALSO BY NC BARTON

The Now in Forever: A Small Town Second Chance Romance

The Art of the Meet Cute: A Small Town Found Family Romance

Coming Soon: Meet Me at the Loch: Book One in the Love on Location Series